Richard H. Wilmer, John Esten Cooke

Hilt to Hilt

Days and nights on the banks of the Shenandoah in the autumn of 1864; from the

mss. of Colonel Surry of Eagle's Nest

Richard H. Wilmer, John Esten Cooke

Hilt to Hilt

Days and nights on the banks of the Shenandoah in the autumn of 1864; from the mss. of Colonel Surry of Eagle's Nest

ISBN/EAN: 9783337381134

Printed in Europe, USA, Canada, Australia, Japan

Cover: Foto ©Andreas Hilbeck / pixelio.de

More available books at **www.hansebooks.com**

HILT TO HILT;

OR,

Days and Nights on the Banks of the Shenandoah

IN THE

AUTUMN OF 1864.

From the Mss. of Colonel Surry of Eagle's Nest.

BY

JOHN ESTEN COOKE,

AUTHOR OF "FAIRFAX," "SURRY OF EAGLE'S NEST," ETC., ETC.

NEW YORK:

G. W. CARLETON, PUBLISHER.

LONDON: S. LOW, SON, & CO.

MDCCCLXIX.

THE NEW YORK PRINTING COMPANY,
81, 83, *and* 85 *Centre Street,*
NEW YORK.

CONTENTS.

CONTENTS.

PROLOGUE.

—◆◆◆—

Colonel Surry to the Reader:

I perform a bold exploit to-day, my dear reader. The exploit in question is sending *Hilt to Hilt* to the press.

It is a long time now since 1866, and, if you have read, you have probably forgotten the volume entitled *Surry of Eagle's Nest*.

Alas! authors must expect to be lost sight of as the years flow on. I am not so vain as to imagine you remember my memoirs; and, for a stronger reason still, you must have forgotten their reception by my critical friends of New England. They were flayed by those fierce foemen. I recall the ceremony with a nervous shiver. Those terrible literary Camanches brandished the tomahawk, uttered the war-whoop, and performed a dance of fearful triumph around the prostrate and bleeding victim.

The unfortunate memoirs of Colonel Surry were "highly-seasoned . . . duels and murderous settlements of deadly feuds kept up the excitement" . . . the author need not fear that his portrait of Stuart would "bore any one fifty years hence," as nobody at that remote period would know of the book's existence . . . parts were "cribbed from Dickens" . . . "it might find a good market with the 'New York Ledger.'" .

. . the style was "so excessively florid, that but for the perpetual flow of incident it would be intolerable!" . . . and "the literary execution was in that exaggerated style in which the Southern writers so often indulge!"

All this, and more, descended on the unfortunate Colonel Surry.

Well, that *bon mot* about "fifty years hence" made me laugh. The phrases "excessively florid" and "exaggerated style" made me reflect. Was I then so very florid and exaggerated, as my friends declared? I had supposed the MS. of *Surry of Eagle's Nest* to have been composed in a most compact, terse, and altogether faultless style; — and here was a great critic, and a critic in Boston, which was worse still, declaring that I was florid and exaggerated!

What to do? Alas! *Surry of Eagle's Nest* was printed. The poor youth had made his entrance into the bustling world, and the mischief was done. I could only resolve that, in future, I would never be florid or exaggerated any more — that I would avoid the errours of the past: another flaying, like that received from the Pilgrim sons of New England, would, I felt, put an end to my career.

In the present episode of my memoirs, therefore, good reader, which I call *Hilt to Hilt*, I tell a plain and unadorned story. I hope the style is not florid; I know the events, strange as they appear, are not exaggerated. It is almost impossible, indeed, to exaggerate the wild romance of that Partisan life of 1864. I have lived in the midst of it; seen it with my eyes; known and spoken with the actors in it; and yet I assure you that I find it difficult to realize that the whole was not a dream.

Let me repeat that whatever seems strangest in this book is substantially, when not literally, true. There were one or two additional incidents which I designed to relate. I have not related them. I felt that the reader would call me a " sensation-writer."

Here, then, worthy reader, I present you with a brief and fierce episode in the strange life of the Virginia border, in the autumn of 1864.

Some of the men who figured in these scenes are dead. Others still live, and will tell you that I exaggerate nothing.

SURRY OF EAGLE'S NEST.

HILT TO HILT.

I.

IN "MOSBY'S CONFEDERACY."

In the first days of autumn, 1864, I left Petersburg, where Lee confronted Grant, to go on a tour of duty to the Shenandoah Valley, where Early confronted Sheridan.

This journey was made on horseback, and I encountered upon the way some curious incidents and remarkable personages.

Incidents and personages suited the epoch: for, strangest of the strange, was that autumn of 1864! Do you remember it, reader? For my part, I shall never forget it. On all sides, doubt, anxiety, suffering, — a sombre defiance mingled with despair. From every quarter, — North, South, East, and West, — the clash of arms; by day and by night, on the four winds, the roar of cannon; in the trenches by the Appomattox, the incessant rattle of skirmishers; in the fields and forests of the border, the crack of pistols and carbines. The war mortal, — breast to

11

breast, hilt to hilt. The country desolate; the fields
untilled; the women in black, weeping for dead hus-
bands; the children in rags, calling for dead fathers!

In that lugubrious autumn of the dark year '64,
the Southern Enceladus was prostrate, and vainly
writhed beneath the mountains piled upon him.
Lee's keen and trenchant rapier was worn to the hilt
nearly; and the red flag, so long borne aloft on its
point, was about to fall, and be dragged in the dust
of defeat; but never, Heaven be thanked, in the mire
of dishonour!

It was at this tragic epoch that I set out on my
horseback journey through Virginia.

Crossing the Rapidan at Raccoon Ford, above
Chancellorsville, and the Rappahannock near the
little village of Orleans, I pushed on through
Fauquier, gazing with curious interest on the
deserted country around me. It was a very different
region from the lowland which I had just left, and
war was evidently carried on here in a very different
fashion. At Petersburg, two great armies faced
each other behind breast-works, — sullen, watchful,
resembling lions about to spring; and these lions
were fed by railroads and long trains of wagons,
going and coming from every quarter. Here, in
Fauquier, at the foot of the mountains, there were
no armies, no railroads, no wagons, and, it seemed,
no troops of any description whatever. "Mosby's

Confederacy," as the people called the region, was
apparently uninhabited. I went on, mile after mile,
without encountering a human being. The roads
were deserted. Stray cattle wandered wild on the
slopes of the great hills. The partridge, long unmolested, and free from all apprehension, perched on
the fence beside me as I passed along, perfectly
tranquil, within a few feet of my pistol's muzzle.

This physiognomy of the landscape, however, did
not deceive me. I knew very well that it was only
the chance of travel which enabled me thus to pass
unchallenged; for this country which I was traversing — like the banks of the Shenandoah — was
notoriously a "Debatable Land," — the home of
the scout and the ranger. On these deserted roads
took place those incessant combats of Mosby and his
men with the Federal cavalry. These forests were
the scenes of those ambuscades, surprises, sudden
collisions, in which sabres clashed, pistols and carbines rang, and yells rose, mingling with the din of
hoofs, as the blue and gray rangers came together.
Not a week passed here but the autumn leaves were
dyed still redder with the blood of human beings.

Such were the scenes and figures which peopled
my imagination as I rode on through the forests of
Fauquier. Under the tranquil beauty there was
something sombre and menacing. I had heard, of
this land, a hundred bloody histories, — the strangest

tales of private feuds and secret vengeances. Here, on the war-harried Virginia border, men had appeared mysteriously, coming, none knew whence; had joined the Partisans under names which were clearly assumed; had fought with deadly rancour; fallen unnoted, and disappeared as the autumn leaf flits away on the wind, swallowed up with their mystery in oblivion. Men hated each other bitterly everywhere, in 1864; but north of the Rappahannock, and along the banks of the Shenandoah, there seemed to be something terrible and bloody in the very atmosphere, which inflamed the heart, and drove to mad excesses all who breathed it.

Such was the Border during the last months of the war; and it is a page from the unpublished history of this strange "place and time" — the banks of the Shenandoah between Winchester and the Blue Ridge, in 1864 — that I beg leave to lay before the reader.

After a day and night at "The Oaks," the residence of my friend, Colonel Beverley, near Markham, I resumed my journey; and, following the mountain road through a gorge of the Blue Ridge, reached about sunset the small village of Paris.

Paris lies, like a hawk's nest, in that gash of the mountain called Ashby's Gap. At that time it might have been compared with more fitness to a sentinel posted to watch the gorge and give the alarm on the approach of an enemy. That enemy frequently made his appearance. Sheridan lay on the Opequon, watching his daring opponent, Early; and scouting parties of Federal cavalry passed and repassed, almost daily, through the gap, on the lookout for Confederates. Like the whole country, Paris appeared poverty-stricken and melancholy. The houses were nearly deserted; the fences had been pulled down; the sign-board of the old tavern was hanging by one corner; the tavern itself was dismantled; grass grew in the streets of the hamlet, and scarce a cur yelped. There is a picture "in little" of a Virginia village in 1864.

In front of the rickety tavern some horses were standing bridled and saddled. On the low fence were sitting several officers and men in gray. Among these I recognized Colonel F——, of General Longstreet's staff, who got down and came to meet me. We exchanged a cordial greeting. I gave him the news from Petersburg, and then asked him in turn for intelligence from the Valley.

"Nothing," was his reply. "Early is still at Winchester, and Sheridan on the Opequon, — afraid to attack."

"How is the country around Millwood, on the other side of the gap?"

"Full of Yankees, with a heavy picket at Berry's Ferry."

This was discouraging, as I wished to go on to the house of a friend near White Post, that evening. To retrace my steps, and enter the Valley by Manassas Gap, seemed absurd.

"I think I'll try and get over somewhere," I said.

"Get over — to-night?" exclaimed the colonel.

"Yes."

"You'll certainly be captured."

"I will risk it."

"Well, good luck to you, my dear fellow. Shake hands: I always like to take affectionate leave of a friend who is about to ' go up.' "

We exchanged a grasp of the hand amid general laughter from the crowd, and my friend went back to his perch on the fence. I turned my horse's head up the mountain.

I had not gone twenty steps when I heard the colonel call after me.

"I say, Surry!"

I turned my head.

"Give my love to any friends of mine you meet *in Washington!* " *

It was with this most cheerful of "last greetings" still ringing in my ears that I went on up the mountain.

* His words.

II.

SLOWLY ascending the steep road, I reached the "Big Poplar," a well-known tree on the summit of the mountain, just as the last rays of sunset were bathing in red and orange the autumn foliage.

From the direction of Winchester came the dull mutter of cannon, and an occasional carbine shot was heard in front from the picket at the ford. All this was in disagreeable contrast with the tranquil beauty of the landscape. The sides of the Gap burned with the first fiery tints of autumn. The blue mountains, melting into haze, rolled far away southward, like gigantic billows. Through the gorge, flushed with sunset, lay the beautiful, the enchanting, the wonderful Valley of the Shenandoah.

It seemed a sacrilege to desecrate this fairy region, — to trample these sweet fields beneath the iron heel of war. But the heel was upon them. The land was a waste. Every pass was guarded. Not even the solitary and inoffensive Surry could get across the mountain to his friends, without imminent danger of capture.

I had determined, however, to attempt it. By flanking the picket in front, and crossing at the private and unused ford, called "The Island," below, I hoped to make my way unperceived to the house of the friend referred to, who lived beyond Millwood.

To the execution of this scheme I now proceeded. Night was rapidly descending, and, by the time I reached the Mount-Carmel road, branching off to my right, it was dark.

I had scarcely gone two hundred yards on the narrow mountain road, half concealed beneath evergreens and overhanging rocks, when all at once a shadow seemed to rise from the earth in front of me. I heard the click of a trigger, and a voice said: —

"Halt! Who goes there?"

"Friend," I replied, cocking my pistol under my cape.

"What command?" said the voice.

"Army of Northern Virginia. What do you belong to?"

"The Night-Hawks," was the reply of the shadow.

A brief silence followed.

"Good!" I said, at length. "I never heard of the Night-Hawks, but I know you are a Virginian from your voice, and from your post on this road. I am going to cross at the Island."

"I will ride with you," said the horseman.

I assented to this at once, and we rode on in the darkness side by side, in silence.

Descending the rugged declivity, we reached the banks of the river, overhung by the white arms of immense sycamores, plunged into the water, and, half fording, half swimming, reached the Island, and then the western bank.

Crossing a small field we entered a forest which seemed uninhabited, except by the owls, whose weird laughter was heard in the thicket, or the whippoor-wills, crying plaintively from the interwoven festoons between the great sycamores. We had scarcely gone fifty steps in the wood, however, when a second shadow rose in the path; challenged, was responded to in a low voice by my companion; and we continued our way.

I have been on dark marches. Once with General Stuart, near Chantilly, in 1862, we rode on through a night so murky that our horses resembled black phantoms breasting a sea of ink. But that ride through the woods of the Shenandoah surpassed all.

All at once, however, a weird light filtrated through the boughs, and I glanced over my shoulder. The moon had just soared above the pine-clad summit of the Blue Ridge, like a great shield bathed in blood.

Then the wood opened before us, and a small glade revealed itself, completely walled in with thickets.

Suddenly I saw the gleam of a red Confederate battle-flag; and in the glade twenty or thirty horses stood fully equipped. Beside them lay their riders, — every man holding his bridle, and ready to mount at a moment's notice.

III.

ERECT, in the centre of the wild and picturesque group, stood a man, leaning one heavily gauntleted hand on the pommel of his saddle, the other on the hilt of a light sabre.

He was apparently about twenty-five or six; and his plain gray coat, buttoned from top to bottom, defined a figure, straight, supple, and vigourous. Around his waist he wore a red sash; his boots reached above the knee; over his forehead drooped a brown hat, with the black cavalry feather. The face, which the moonlight clearly revealed, was a striking one. In the penetrating eyes, and the lips, half covered with a shaggy moustache, could be read something cool, resolute, and "thorough-bred." Never was *will* written plainer on human countenance. This man evidently belonged to that class who think, decide, and act for themselves, preserving through all an invincible coolness. In the face, for the rest, there was something hard and impassive. One glance at him convinced me that he had passed through some terrible ordeal, and had come out, steel.

I was sure that I had seen him somewhere; but was completely at a loss to determine where or when.

I approached with my companion.

" Who is that?" he said, in the brief tone of command.

He glanced at me keenly. Then all at once, before my friend of the Mount-Carmel road could reply, the Partisan added coolly: —

" I am glad to see you, Colonel Surry!"

With which words he advanced a step, made me the bow of a nobleman, and, drawing off his yellow gauntlet, offered me his hand.

" Ah! you know me, captain!" I said, taking the hand, which was white and slender, but had the grip of a vice.

" Perfectly, colonel; I have had the pleasure of seeing you in the army."

Suddenly I remembered.

" And I have seen you, captain. It was near Manassas last October, when the cavalry followed Meade after Bristoe. We came to a barricade near Yates' ford; the leading squadron wavered before the volleys of the sharpshooters; *you* took the front, charged over the felled trees, and drove the enemy. General Stuart paid you a magnificent compliment on that occasion, and never was one better deserved, — Captain St. Leger!"

The partisan gave me one of his penetrating glances.

"My name is Landon, colonel," he said, with perfect calmness.

I looked at him with undisguised astonishment.

"And yet I could swear it was *you* that made that charge! Is it possible that two human beings can resemble each other so strangely?"

For a moment he made no reply. He was evidently hesitating.

"You were not that officer?" I said.

"Well, yes, colonel, the officer in question was myself, and at that time I was called St. Leger. I have since resumed my real name, or rather the full name of which the former was a portion."

"Your real name?"

"St. Leger Landon, at your service," returned the Partisan, coolly, and making me a bow.

Before I could reply, our colloquy was brought suddenly to an end.

"All right, captain!" said a low voice, behind the Partisan.

And a boy of about sixteen, mild, fair-haired, and gentle in appearance, advanced noiselessly into the area.

"Touch-and-go!" said the partisan, "well, how many?"

"Seventy or eighty, captain."

"That is three horses apiece for the command! Lieutenant Arden."

A young man of about twenty-two rose quickly from among the prostrate figures, and approached, saluting. There was something gay and gallant in his sparkling eyes and smiling lips, but what chiefly impressed me was the singular sweetness and modesty of his bearing and expression.

Landon introduced me to the young lieutenant; gave him some rapid orders, and then turned to me.

"I am going to attack the picket at the river, colonel, — will you look on?"

"I will do better, captain, — take a hand, — if I am allowed to rank as a Night-Hawk, and keep the fresh horse I capture."

"You shall keep half a dozen if you choose, colonel."

And Landon vaulted into the saddle with an ease which showed the perfect horseman, the thorough cavalier, who would stop at nothing.

"Attention!"

Before the sound of his voice had died away, every man was in the saddle.

"Unfurl the flag!"

The order was obeyed.

Then, as silently as though they had been a party of phantoms, the little band began to move beneath the shadowy foliage toward the picket.

IV.

THE little band of Night-Hawks had gone about half a mile, when, through an opening in the forest, we caught a gleam from the moonlit river.

On the bank, beneath some great sycamores, was a dusky and confused group of men and horses. From this group rose a stifled hum.

All at once, Touch-and-go laid his hand upon Landon's arm.

"Hist! captain," he whispered; "you are almost on the vidette."

"Where is he?"

"Just beyond that thicket."

"Can you capture him without noise?"

Touch-and-go made a silent movement with his head.

"I will halt, then," said Landon. And with a gesture he halted the column.

Touch-and-go had dismounted; had gone forward stealthily on foot; and not a sound was heard.

Five minutes passed thus; then two figures

25

emerged from the shadow : it was Touch-and-go with his prisoner.

"Good!" said Landon. "You don't make much noise."

"I put my pistol to his head, and he surrendered without a word."

Landon turned to the prisoner, a black-browed individual in blue, and was about to speak, when one of the horses of the party uttered a shrill neigh.

"Look out, captain," said Touch-and-go, in a low voice, "that will put them on their guard."

"Right!" exclaimed Landon, and, drawing his sabre, he struck the spur into his horse, and shouted, "Charge!"

The column swept forward like a storm-wind, and fell with loud yells on the picket, which ran hastily to horse. It was too late. Landon's men were in the midst of them, banging with the pistol and slashing with the sabre.

It was a scene of the wildest confusion, and nothing was heard but shouts, groans, and yells. The officer commanding the Federal picket attempted vainly to rally his men. They fled wildly from the river, over the road to Millwood, with the Rangers pressing them at every step. That moonlight surprise and chase was singular. I will always remember it; and nothing remains so distinctly in my mind as the figure of Landon, as he rushed upon the track of the officer commanding the Federals.

Landon had seemed to disdain all other opponents, and evidently sought this one alone. When the Federal officer followed his flying picket, the Partisan singled him out, drove his horse onward on the track of the fugitive, with bloody spurs; and when within sight of Millwood, just above a mill, I saw him come up with his adversary.

As the Partisan reached his side, the sabres gleamed in the moon, and a ringing clash followed. Landon had delivered the "right cut;" his weapon had encountered his opponent's guard; the Partisan's sabre was shivered.

He dropped the stump, drew his pistol, and fired every barrel, with the muzzle resting almost on the Federal officer's breast. Every charge missed; the speed of the horses was so great that no human aim could be relied on.

Suddenly a loud cheer was heard from the direction of Millwood; a din of smiting hoofs mingled with it, and the long continuous splash of a column passing through a little stream in front, indicated that a heavy reinforcement of Federal cavalry, alarmed by the firing, was pressing forward.

They were not three hundred yards distant; their drawn sabres flashed in the moonbeams. As well as I could make out, they numbered about two hundred men.

Landon had just fired his last barrel, when the enemy came on at a headlong gallop. I saw a flash dart from the Partisan's eye; his white teeth gnawed the under lip. Burying both rowels in the sides of his horse, he was, in an instant, beside the Federal officer of the picket, and, raising his pistol, struck him with the weapon over the head.

The blow was enough to fell an ox. The officer dropped his rein, fell from the saddle, and, his foot hanging in the stirrup, was dragged onward by his flying animal, and disappeared.

At the same instant, from the leading platoon of the Federal cavalry, came a shower of bullets. Landon coolly snapped his empty pistol in their faces, turned his horse, and, galloping down the declivity to the mill, drew up his men upon the slope just beyond, to receive the Federal charge.

It came and swept all before it. For a moment the air was full of pistol and carbine shots, clashing blades and resounding shouts. Then Landon's men were driven with the sabre. With the enemy close upon their heels, banging and slashing, the Night-Hawks retreated rapidly past the débouchement of the Bethel road, toward the Shenandoah.

This was the position of affairs, when, by one of those sudden incidents, which render Partisan combats so exciting, the whole face of things was changed.

Landon had been swept back more than half a mile; had leaped the stone fence on the side of the turnpike, and was pouring a hot fire into the enemy's flank, as they charged by, when, suddenly, rapid firing, accompanied by loud shouts, was heard in the Federal rear. At that sound, the leading squadron paused, half undecided. Landon decided them. Leaping into the road with ten or fifteen men he made an obstinate charge, the Federals gave back, and, extending his arm, Landon uttered a shout of fierce triumph.

I followed the direction of his finger. The crest at the mouth of the Bethel road was swarming with gray horsemen, at least a hundred, apparently, in number. They had fallen on the Federal rear; were now firing and cutting among them; and it was scarcely ten minutes before the entire force of blue horsemen was retreating, hotly pursued, through the village of Millwood, toward Berryville.

Never was work done better or more rapidly. The Federal horse were swept away as leaves are swept by the wind. The sudden surprise had completely "demoralized" them, — a misfortune which will occur, under such circumstances, to all but the best troops; and the combat had become a mere fox-chase.

My horse was killed under me as I was passing

the mill in pursuit; but I had only to mount one of twenty which were running about riderless.

Seizing a fine bay by the bridle, I threw myself into the saddle, and soon rejoined Landon, beyond Millwood. He had given up further pursuit, sent to recall his men, and was sitting his horse in the middle of the turnpike.

"The dead go fast," I heard him mutter, as I rode to his side. "I wonder if it was that wretch, or his ghost?"

V.

CAPTAIN BLOUNT.

THE officer who had come so opportunely to our assistance was Captain Blount, one of the most daring Partisans of the war.

I had met Captain Blount incidentally in 1863, and, as we slowly rode back now together toward Millwood, I looked with interest at a man of whom I had heard so much.

He appeared to be between twenty-five and thirty; his figure was graceful; his seat in the saddle perfect; his countenance full of unassuming courtesy, and the expression of his eyes soft, pensive, almost sad. It was difficult to recognize in this mild and retiring personage, so cordial and gentle, the hero of a hundred desperate encounters. Of his skill as a swordsman, I had, however, witnessed a striking evidence. In the pursuit through Millwood he had crossed swords with a Federal officer who was evidently an accomplished *sabreur;* fought hilt to hilt with him, in single combat, for nearly ten minutes; and finally killed his adversary by driving his sabre, at tierce point, through him from breast to back. The officer had thown up his arms, reeled and fallen. Blount continued the pursuit; only his sabre was bloody.

Returning now, after this hard work, nothing could be imagined more simple and unassuming than his bearing. But a spectacle which greeted us near the village made the mild eye flash. The Federal troopers had picketed their horses to the fence around the grounds of the little church, nestling amid its green trees, laid waste the grounds, broken open the sacred edifice, and torn to pieces the organ.

Blount looked at the broken door of the church, the torn-down pews, and the fragments of the organ scattered over the lawn.

"These are Scythians, indeed!" he muttered, quoting the words of Napoleon; "there is nothing to do but to hunt down and kill every mam of them."

"A maxim which you religiously carry out, Blount," said Landon; "but how did you happen to arrive in such good time to-night?"

"By accident, my dear Landon. I was going on a scout along the Opequon, when I heard the firing, and thought it was you. I am glad I was near; and, as the affair is over now, I believe I will go on."

Having uttered these words in his mild and courteous voice, Captain Blount offered me his hand, gave me a cordial invitation to visit him when it was convenient, and, after exchanging a pressure of the hand with Landon, moved off with his squadron of about seventy-five men toward the Opequon.

I was still looking after the retreating shadows, when one of the Partisans rode up, leading a magnificent bay.

"Here is the Yankee officer's horse, captain, — the one you knocked out of the saddle," he said.

Landon glanced at the animal.

"They must have carried off the captain, but he has left his horse and his papers," said the man.

"His papers?" said Landon, quickly.

The man pointed to the saddle-pockets, and drew forth a bundle of official documents.

Landon rapidly tore them open, and glanced at them by the light of the moon. His face was lost in the shadow, and I did not see its expression.

"Then it was not his ghost," muttered the Partisan; "and he is not dead, after all!"

3

VI.

HOW THEY MANAGED MATTERS ON THE BORDER IN 1864.

LANDON had turned his horse to ride down the hill, in the direction of the village, when one of his men came up rapidly, and, drawing rein at his side, spoke to him in a low voice.

I did not catch the words, but the blood rushed suddenly to Landon's cheek.

"Where?" he said, abruptly.

"In the flat beyond the stream, captain."

Without a word Landon darted at full gallop down the hill, passed through Millwood, and, as I reached his side in the field beyond, I saw him check his horse suddenly near an oak, which stood, solitary and alone, in the open ground.

From the boughs of this oak were hanging three corpses.

"Look, captain," said the man who had kept beside him; "it is Robinson, Walters, and Andrews, — three of our best men."

Landon spurred his horse up until the animal shied violently at this near approach to the fearful-looking objects. The three men were clad in gray, and their ghastly faces were convulsed by the last agony.

Suddenly Landon forced his horse close to the trunk, and tore down a paper which was attached to it.

On this paper was written, in heavy black letters : —

> "Such is the fate of the Night-Hawks.
> "By command of
> "CAPT. RATCLIFFE."

Landon read these words by the light of the moon, looked up at the corpses, folded up the paper slowly, and, turning to the man beside him, said : —

"Order my command to assemble here, and bring the prisoners taken from the picket at the river."

I had reached his side as he uttered these words, and he held out to me the paper which he had taken from the tree-trunk.

"It is frightful," I said; "and what course will you pursue, captain?"

With an icy glance the Partisan replied : —

"The *lex talionis* is my code, colonel, — an eye for an eye, and a tooth for a tooth."

As he spoke, the members of his command were seen approaching, with about a dozen prisoners.

VII.

AN EYE FOR AN EYE.

DEATH in battle is one thing; it seems natural. Death by a military execution is another thing, and seems unnatural, repulsive, and horrible. One stirs the pulses, for it is tragic and terrible. The other revolts the feelings, for it is disgusting.

Other considerations induce me to omit a minute account of the fierce spectacle which I witnessed that night. "Melodrama! — claptrap!" some good people would be apt to exclaim. And for fear of these terrible critics, it behoves those who write their own adventures to consult the *vraisemblable* rather than the *vrai*.

These things occurred, and will not be believed. Let me therefore pass rapidly over the event of that night of 1864.

The prisoners were ranged in a line with the men of the band opposite, and Landon sat his horse looking at the former. His face was perfectly calm, and he did not utter a word. When the preparations had been made, and a sergeant had reported with finger to his hat, Landon turned to me.

"Colonel Surry," he said, "I am glad you are
here to-night and can testify to what you witness. I
am a regularly commissioned officer in the Confederate States army; my command is a regularly
enrolled company under the Partisan Ranger Act
of the Confederate Congress; I make open war on
the enemy, under the Confederate flag; and I and
my men are treated, not as open enemies, but as
bandits. You see before you a proof of this assertion. The three men hanging yonder were among
the best and bravest of my command. They went
out yesterday, — in Confederate uniform, as you see,
— to attack a wagon-train belonging to Sheridan's
army, were taken prisoners, and are hung here by
Captain Ratcliffe, of the Federal cavalry, as guerillas. I have captured to-night a dozen men from
Ratcliffe's command: they stand before you. What
is necessary to protect my men hereafter from being
thus murdered in cold blood?"

There was but one reply to make.

"The death of three of these prisoners," I said.

"You are right, colonel. I am glad we agree."

And, tearing a leaf from his despatch-book, Landon wrote upon it some lines; the bright moonlight
enabled him to do so without difficulty. He then
turned to Arden.

"Lieutenant," he said, "you will see to the execution of the following orders. These prisoners

will proceed to draw lots; three will thus be designated, and these three will be allowed fifteen minutes to perform their devotions, after which they will be shot to death. You will then take down the bodies hanging yonder, remove them to Millwood, where they will be placed in coffins, to await my return to-morrow, and the bodies of the three prisoners will be hung in the places which my men now occupy. Lastly, you will affix to the trunk of the tree beneath them the paper which I hold in my hand. It contains the words : —

"'These three men of Captain Ratcliffe's command are executed by my order, in retaliation for three of my own men, murdered in cold blood by himself.

"'St. Leger Landon,

"'*Captain C. S. A.*'"

Arden saluted and received the paper from the hand of Landon.

"For the performance of this duty," continued the Partisan, "you will detail six men, and will see in person that my orders are executed. When performed, report to me at the Bethel Cross Roads, where I will bivouac."

There was something terribly weird in these business-like and commonplace details of a bloody tragedy. Landon gave his orders with the air of a man who is merely following a routine as humdrum as guard-mounting, or calling the roll.

His voice was unmoved; his countenance perfectly indifferent. Having finished, he turned his horse's head toward the river, and we rode off together, followed by the whole command, with the exception of the six men who remained with Arden.

I was only too glad to leave the spot. The terrible scene about to be enacted had no attractions in my eyes, — thoroughly as I approved it, — and I turned my back upon the gloomy locality with a long breath of relief.

Landon exhibited no emotion of any description. His impassive countenance revealed nothing. Riding in silence past the mill, where he paused a few moments to look after the wounded carried thither, and to give orders for their transfer in safety beyond the Ridge, he turned into the road by which Blount had come to his assistance, and, going half a mile, halted in a little wood near a cross roads.

Suddenly, as the column halted, three shots resounded from the direction of Millwood. I could not suppress a shudder at that sound, which indicated that three human beings had passed from time to eternity.

I looked at Landon. His countenance was entirely unmoved.

"Put out videttes," he said, in a calm voice, to a sergeant, "and tell the men to unsaddle."

Half an hour afterwards I had wrapped my cape around me, and fallen asleep, worn out with fatigue, beneath a tree.

Such were the events of my first night on the Shenandoah.*

* This incident is real.

VIII.

THE beams of the September sun, darting from the summit of the Blue Ridge, and turning the dewy leaves to molten gold, awoke me.

Landon was already up, and the men were busy around their bivouac fires, preparing breakfast. It was a plain but excellent meal, and having finished I rose to depart.

"Then you will not stay and attend the burial of my poor fellows to-night, colonel?"

"The burial to-night, captain?"

"Yes, I regard it as a duty I owe them. They were brave and faithful soldiers, and deserve something more than to be thrown into the first ditch by the roadside. God willing, no man of my command shall be thus treated; and I intend to bury these three in the Old Chapel graveyard, about three miles from Millwood, on the road to Berryville. I should like to do so by daylight; but a strong force is camped near the Chapel, and it is impossible."

"You will go to-night?"

41

"To-night, and as quietly as possible. Will you accompany us?"

The expedition strangely attracted me. That love of adventure which all men possess, surrounded this nocturnal march in the performance of a pious duty, with an irresistible charm.

"I will go with you, captain," I said, "but will first make a visit to a friend near White Post. Will I find you here at sunset?"

"Then, or soon afterwards. I am going on a reconnoissance toward the Chapel, and will have returned by that time."

"Good! I will be punctual." And, exchanging a pressure of the hand with my host, I set off to make my visit.

That visit has no connection with the present history, and I shall not dwell upon it. Punctually at sunset I was again in sight of the cross roads, and found the command, with the exception of Landon and one or two of the men, at the same spot in the woods which they had occupied on the preceding night.

The scene was picturesque. The red light of sunset fell upon a little glade in the forest, and, grouped beneath a tall oak, with their horses ready saddled, and picketed to the boughs around, the Rangers had surrendered themselves to the social delights of the bivouac.

At the moment, the attention of all was centred upon Lieutenant Arden, who, seated upon a root of the oak, with his back against the trunk, was playing upon a banjo, and singing.

I had heard the music commence just as I turned a corner of the road, and the words came clearly to me on the calm evening air. Determined not to interrupt the singer, I checked my horse, remained motionless, and listened.

I should have expected some rude camp ballad in this bivouac of the Rangers — or, if Arden sang, some stirring war lyric, full of the clash of the sabre, the bang of carbines, and the ring of the bugle. What I heard was very different; and, strangest of all, was listened to by the Rangers with obvious sympathy and admiration. The song which the young *sabreur* sang — this youth who had proved himself a veritable firebrand on the preceding evening, cutting more than one man out of the saddle — was the following : —

" ARDEN'S SONG.

" On the Shenandoah the rose is in bloom,
    And the oriole sings in the sycamore-tree ;
    And Annie — I ask myself all the day long —
    If Annie is thinking of me !

" Alone in my tent on the Rapidan,
    I fancy the wind in the dreamy pines
  Is the sigh of the mountain evergreens
    By the ford in the Yankee lines !

" Bloom on, sweet roses of other years !
　 Sing, oriole gay, in the sycamore-tree !
　 Past the Rapidan and the Blue Ridge wave
　　 Is the face that I long to see !

" Ring out, silver bugle, the signal of strife !
　 Spur, sabre, and stirrup, clank merry and free !
　 To horse ! I am coming ! — and then I shall know
　　 If Annie is dreaming of me ! "

As the sweet and tender accents of the youthful voice died away, I cried " Bravo ! " and the Rangers started up. I approached, and received a cordial greeting; after which Lieutenant Arden made room for me on the root beside him, and I requested him to go on.

" I was only singing the boys a little song of mine," he said, with a blush and a laugh; "they pretend that they like it, but their real favorites are ' Johnny, fill up the Bowl,' and ' Jine the Cavalry.' "

With these words, Arden handed the banjo to one of the men, who sang in succession that lively ditty, commencing : —

" We were ordered to charge and not to stop,
　 And we charged right into a whiskey shop !
　　 We'll all drink stone blind,
　　 Johnny, fill up the bowl ! "

And then the famous song, so loved by Stuart : —

" If you want to have a good time,
   Jine the cavalry !
      Bully boys, hey ! "

Have you ever heard those wonderful lyrics, my
dear reader ?   If not, I should like to quote them,
which I assure you I could do without missing a
single word.   I should like especially to record the
latter, that great comic Iliad of the *sabreurs* of
Stuart ; to lay before you in full, the most popular
of all the cavalry ballads of the war.   But, alas ! to
give the mere words would be to offer you a withered
flower, from which the colour and perfume had fled.
It would be nothing — this famous ditty — without
the tune, without the banjo, without the foliage above,
and the fires of the bivouac glimmering near.

The performer executed it admirably, and the Rangers joined rapturously in the chorus.   The woods
rang ; the very horses turned their heads, and the
men starting to their feet, began to dance to the up-
roarious strumming, above which rose the gay cavalry chorus.   Altogether the scene was indescribable
for its grotesque merriment ; the Rangers had surrendered themselves to a mirth which passed all
bounds.

It was in the very midst of the revelry that the
sound of horses' hoofs was heard, and Landon appeared at the turn of the road, accompanied by
Touch-and-go.   As Arden saw him, he extended his

hand toward the performer on the banjo, buckled on his sabre, and gave the order : —

" Prepare to mount ! "

At that command the merriment ceased as if by magic. The men ran to their horses, and, at a second order from Arden, mounted and formed column. The young man then rode up to Landon, made the military salute, and said : —

" Ready, captain ! "

Landon saluted in return, pressed my hand cordially, and, running his keen eye along the column, placed himself at the head, and gave successively the orders : —

" Unfurl the flag ! " and " Forward ! "

The red flag was unfurled, the column moved, and, at a steady pace, went back over the road by which we had reached the bivouac on the preceding evening.

Ere long the houses of Millwood appeared, embowered in trees, and, in the waste ground in front, rose the great oak.

As we passed, I turned my head, and looked at it. From the boughs, in place of the dead Confederates, hung the three Federal cavalrymen executed on the preceding evening. Against the trunk of the tree something glimmered in the moonlight. It was the paper stating the grounds upon which the death penalty had been inflicted.

Habituated as I had long been to the horrours of war, the three ghastly figures were appalling. There was something gloomy and lugubrious in their outlines, as they dangled from the great oak, illumined by the moon; the spectacle was tragic and terrible.

As Landon rode by, I saw him look at them, and tried to discover in his countenance some traces of emotion. There were none whatever. He gazed at the ghastly figures with an expression of entire indifference, and his face had the cold, hard look which characterized it invariably when in repose. Was there any feeling under that mask? I know not. Men's faces are bad indices. Suffering hardens, and stamps a gloomy impress on the very muscles at length; and under that frozen surface thoughts come and go as the tide does beneath the ice, without moving the hard crust.

Landon rode on without uttering a word, and passing through the little stream, over which some tall trees leaned, we entered the village of Millwood, which the superb moonlight bathed in its mellow splendour.

The bodies of the three Confederates awaited us in rude pine coffins, deposited in a light wagon ready to move. On the coffins some young ladies had placed wreaths and garlands of autumn flowers; and, as we appeared, more than one fair figure, glimmering in the moonlight, raised a white handkerchief to her eyes; more than one sob was uttered by those standing beside the coffins.

Landon saluted, but did not open his lips. At a sign from him, the men ranged themselves in front; the wagon moved; and the funeral cortege, with the red flag borne in front, ascended the hill, proceeding slowly in the direction of the Old Chapel.

I shall never forget that strange night march. The little band of Rangers, going to bury their dead comrades by moonlight, presented a solemn and moving spectacle, and the landscape was in unison with the occasion. The chill wind of the September night sighed through the great oaks, and the moon shone with a dreamy and memorial splendour, lighting up the highway, the trees, the modest little church on its grassy slope, and the hamlet nestling down behind us, amid the autumn foliage. The band moved slowly on; scarce a hoof-stroke was heard; and the men resembled rather so many silent phantoms than human beings. It was, in truth, a strange scene, and a stranger errand. We were going thus, under cover of darkness, to give our poor, dead comrades Christian burial in holy ground, because we could not do so by day, for fear of interruption. Even now, amid the shadows of night, it was possible that some eye would spy us; some enemy interrupt us — and then we must fight. A fight over graves! The living must fall, that the dead might be buried! — the dead burying the dead!

We entered a forest, emerged into the open country beyond, and, ascending a lofty hill, were within a mile of the chapel.

"I think we will have to fight, colonel," said Landon, by whose side I was riding. "There is a heavy force of cavalry just this side of Berryville, and a picket at the Chapel. I reconnoitred this morning in person."

"In that case you will attack?"

"Yes, I am determined to bury my poor fellows yonder in spite of them."

As Landon spoke, a shot was heard in front, and then another quickly following the first.

"That is bad," said the Partisan. "Touch-and-go must have run into them unawares."

"You sent him on ahead?"

"Yes, to discover if any change had taken place in the position of the picket."

And, turning round, Landon said in his clear, low voice : —

"Halt the column."

At the word it halted, the men remaining motionless on the slope.

All at once muffled hoof-strokes were heard approaching across the wide field on our left. Then a figure appeared advancing on a fleet horse in the dim

4

light. It was Touch-and-go, and in an instant he was beside Landon.

"Well?" said the latter, briefly.

"No change in the picket, captain," was the low reply of the scout; "it is still on the hill above the Chapel."

"You ran into the outer picket?"

"Against one of the videttes, captain. He was completely hidden in the sycamores near the Chapel fence, within a hundred yards of the main body, and before I knew it he fired on me."

"Unlucky."

"Sorry, captain, but really I could not help it. Who would have expected to find a *vidette* hidden there?"

And an expression of quiet contempt came to Touch-and-go's face.

"He fired, and turned to run back; but I put a bullet through him, and he threw up his arms. I then jumped the fence, and came back to report."

Landon reflected an instant.

"You turned to the left?"

"Yes, captain."

"Good! that will do. I will attack in front, and from the right yonder. Lieutenant Arden!"

The young lieutenant rode up and saluted.

"I am going to attack the picket, lieutenant. You will take twelve men and gain that wood yonder on our right, so as to be able to strike the enemy in flank and rear. I will go on, on this road. The signal of your attack will be firing in front. Move quickly, but quietly. I shall break them by a charge with the sabre, and expect to meet you on the hill, lieutenant, when we will drive them."

" All right, captain ; it shall be done."

And, with an animated face, the young officer returned to his men, took twelve, and moved off rapidly, but silently, over the field on the right.

Landon then rode forward, inviting me to follow him.

" Arden will require a little time," he said ; " and we will take a look at the ground, colonel. It is picturesque."

We had left the highway, on both sides of which the fences were torn down, and the turf over which we advanced gave back no echo. Five minutes' ride brought us to the summit of a hill, and from this hill we had a view of the Old Chapel, which lay immediately in front of us.

It was an ancient edifice of plain gray stone nestling in a sort of amphitheatre of hills, dotted with country seats. Near it ran a little stream skirted with sycamores, which extended also upon each side of the highway, forming a vault of foliage above. Beyond the sycamores some weeping willows waved their tassels in the wind, and beneath these glimmered in the moonlight the white tombstones of the tranquil country graveyard.

It seemed like a blot upon the lovely landscape, — that dusky mass of horsemen on the hill beyond. Upon this commanding point the officer of the picket had taken up his position, to observe the main highway over which we were advancing, and a second road, which, forking at the Chapel, ran across our left, in the direction of White Post.

Landon gazed in silence for some moments toward the picket.

"The very worst place I know for an attack," he said; "but I count on Arden, — and my first charge will drive them. Come, colonel," he added, turning his horse rapidly, "I never see such game as is yonder before us, on the hill, without feeling like giving the view-halloo!"

"You are far from complimentary, captain," I said laughing; "you compare our friends to foxes."

"You are right, colonel," said Landon; "they are wolves."

IX.

In a few minutes we had rejoined the band. At a sign from Landon the men moved obliquely into the grassy field where the turf muffled the hoof-strokes and sound of wheels.

"No noise," said Landon, in a low tone; "wait for the word."

And, placing himself in front, he drew his sabre, and advanced rapidly toward the Chapel.

Suddenly, as they approached the sycamore screen near the low fence, a blue horseman, evidently an officer, galloped out, and cried : —

"What command is that ? "

"I will show you," returned Landon.

And, with a whirl of the sabre, he shouted : —

"Charge ! "

At the word the men uttered a yell, dug the spur into their horses, and, passing like a tornado beneath the vault of foliage, rushed up the hill, firing a volley as they did so into the picket. They then closed in with the sabre, and an obstinate combat, hand to hand, followed. It was a weird affair.

53

The moonlight lit up every figure, and the very expressions of the combatants' faces were clearly visible as they fought hilt to hilt.

Landon had only half surprised them, and nothing but his desperate fighting made the result doubtful. The enemy were closing around him; his horse, shot through the head, was staggering, and on the point of hurling his rider beneath the trampling hoofs, when suddenly a volley resounded from the enemy's rear, and Arden, at the head of his horsemen, darted upon them with the drawn sabre.

The result was such as almost invariably follows a surprise. The Federal cavalry gave back, scattered in every direction, and retreated, pursued by the Partisans, at whose head was Landon, mounted on a captured horse, and cutting down everything in his path.

The pursuit continued for half a mile, when a shrill whistle resounded, and the men quickly drew rein. That whistle was Landon's signal, as it was Colonel Mosby's, to "rally on the Chief," as is the cavalry phrase.

In a few minutes the larger portion of the band had assembled on the hill near the Chapel, and every man was accompanied by horses and prisoners.

Landon called to Arden, and the young man hastened up.

"Send the prisoners and horses to the rear, without delay, lieutenant, and detail a party to dig the graves!" he said.

Arden saluted, and rapidly issued the necessary orders, after which he galloped back.

"Deploy the men as skirmishers, and take charge of the left, Arden," the Partisan said; "I will stay on the right. We are going to be attacked, as the alarm is given by this time at the camp of the brigade. Be steady, Arden; hold your ground I am not going away from here until my men are buried!"

"You can count on me, captain!" exclaimed the youth.

"I know it."

And Landon drew up his men on the hill, the delighted Arden hastening off to take command of those on the left.

What followed, exhibited the discernment of the Partisan. In twenty minutes a dark mass appeared coming from the direction of Berryville, and all along the line of sharpshooters resounded the crack of carbines.

From the summit of the hill I then witnessed a curious — what the novelists would call a "dramatic" — spectacle. In the graveyard, near the great weeping willows, I could perceive the dusky figures of the men digging the graves of their dead comrades, while from the field in front came the

incessant report of fire-arms.   The enemy were feeling their way, not knowing the force opposed to
them, and evidently fearing an ambuscade.   Their
advance was thus slow, and the steady fire kept up
along his whole front by Landon, evidently puzzled
them.   Nearly an hour thus passed.   Finally a man
rode up from the graveyard, and reported that the
graves were finished.

"Good!" exclaimed Landon; and galloping to
the spot where Arden was fighting, he said: —

"Keep up a steady fire, lieutenant, and if you
are forced back, retire slowly.   I will be back in
fifteen minutes."

And, requesting me to follow, he turned his horse
and went at a gallop back to the graveyard, the low
wall of which his horse cleared at a bound.   The
graves were dug; the three coffins lay beside them.
It was a singular interment I was about to witness
on this moonlight night, with that incessant report
of carbines resounding beyond the crest; those
bullets rattling against the gray old church, or hissing angrily through the pendant tassels of the weeping willows.

Landon threw himself from his horse and looked
at the graves.   They were wide and deep.

"Good!" he said; "are the ropes ready?"

"All ready, captain," replied one of the men.

"Lower the coffins!"

The ropes were rapidly inserted beneath them, and the three coffins deposited in the graves.

Landon had folded his arms, and an expression of profound sadness veiled the clear light of his dark eyes. Turning to me, he said : —

"This is hard, colonel. Those people yonder grudge us even the few feet of earth we occupy in death ; and we are obliged to bury our brave comrades thus at night, and by stealth. But I do my best, — the soldier's salute will be fired over their graves. God will pardon us, I hope, for having no funeral service read, seeing that we are fighting yonder to keep off the enemy."

" I will read the service," said a low voice behind us.

X.

I TURNED quickly.

Within three paces stood a young lady of slender
and graceful figure, exquisitely fair complexion,
large, brilliant eyes, and dark auburn hair, a few
stray ringlets of which escaped from one of those
small, round hats worn in 1864.

The figure drooped; the eyes were swimming
in tears; but there was something calm and proud
in the countenance, which indicated an entire absence of anything like fear.

For an instant every one gazed at her in silence.
How could she have reached that spot without our
knowledge? A glance indicated all. Upon a flat
tombstone, half hidden behind the trunk of the willow, lay a veil. It was evident that the young lady
had witnessed all from that spot, the drooping leaves
of the weeping willow concealing her.

"I will read the burial service," she said, in a
low voice, and advancing toward the graves. "I
have my prayer-book, and am not afraid."

There was something proud and tranquil in those

58

low tones; and the voice, like the face, made a profound impression upon me.

I looked at Landon. He had become extremely pale, but exhibited, otherwise, no emotion.

Making the young lady a profound bow, he said, with frigid courtesy : —

"I thank you, Miss Adair; this is an unexpected meeting."

"Yes, sir, my appearance no doubt astonished you," came in the same calm tone, though the bullets were whistling above; "and yet it is easily explained. You are aware that I live near, and this evening I walked down by moonlight to visit the Chapel. When the fight took place I stayed, and when the men begun to dig the graves for these poor soldiers, I thought I might be allowed to read the service over them. Was I wrong, sir? 'Tis little for a woman to do for her defenders."

Landon listened to these words in the profoundest silence; but it was easy to see from his compressed lips that he was the prey of bitter emotion.

"Thanks, madam," he said, when she had finished, and saluting as coldly as before. "I accept your offer."

For an instant she did not move, and her eyes were riveted to his countenance.

"Captain Landon," she said, at length, "I wish to speak to you for a moment."

And she walked away from the group, Landon following. When they had gone a few paces, I heard her say to him, in a low voice : —

"You look at me very coldly : why do you do so ? We cannot be friends, but we need not be enemies. I have no bitterness in my heart. I have forgotten the past. At the graves of these poor dead, I pardon all."

"Ah! Miss Adair has forgotten; she pardons!"

The low words were accompanied by a harsh laugh, full of bitter irony.

"From my heart," was the sad reply.

Landon rose to his full stature, and, in a voice full of coldness, almost of sarcasm, said : —

"Miss Adair is too good."

The young lady's head rose suddenly erect at these words, and I read in her face, covered now with a deep flush, an expression of hauteur which surpassed that of her companion.

"Enough, sir!" she said; "I will not further annoy you."

And, turning from him, she was about to leave the spot. All at once, however, her eyes fell upon the coffins — the graves. That spectacle seemed to melt all her pride, and drive away every trace of anger. She stopped — gazed at the coffins — then her head sank, and I heard a low sob issue from her lips.

"Why do you speak to me so?" she murmured,

hurriedly, turning to Landon. "Is it kind? Is it courteous? Should not I speak thus to you, rather? I knew a St. Leger Landon, once, who — alas! war has changed you, sir."

And she covered her eyes with her hand.

Before Landon could reply, a cheer rang beyond the crest. A shower of bullets whistled above us. The enemy were evidently advancing.

"Miss Adair will pardon me," said the Partisan, coldly, "but I must bury my comrades; all is ready."

She replied by a calm inclination, raised a hand-kerchief to her eyes, and in a moment they had returned to the graves.

Then I witnessed a strange and moving spectacle, which I shall never forget, — a young girl was reading by moonlight the burial service over the dead. The pen is powerless to depict the pathetic scene, and I should like to be a painter to place those figures upon canvas, — the rudely clad Partisans, bareheaded, and leaning upon their carbines; Landon, with folded arms, and chin resting on his breast; at the head of the graves, the delicate girl with the ringlets falling upon her shoulders, the pure eyes fixed upon the book from which she was reading, the lips unagitated by the least tremour as she slowly uttered the sublime words of that unapproachable burial service of the Episcopal Church. Imagine these figures grouped in the moonlight, with the weeping willow for a background, by those "unknown graves," as they are called to-day, add the hiss of bullets, the shouts from the crest of the hill, and you will have formed some idea of the scene on that September night.

The young lady's voice did not tremble; her bearing never lost its sweet composure. At last the burial service terminated, and the musical accents died away. Then the earth rattled on the coffins, quick hands filled the graves, and the three mounds rounded beneath the spade.

Scarcely had the work been completed, when a mounted man came at full gallop down the hill, and hastened to the side of Landon.

"Well!" said the latter, in his brief tones.

"The enemy are driving us, captain. Lieutenant Arden told me to say that they are two or three regiments at least, and he won't be able to hold his ground more than ten minutes!"

"Good! say I am coming!" And Landon leaped on his horse. All at once his eye fell upon the young lady, and he paused. Then he said, quietly:—

"Colonel Surry, will you oblige me by conducting Miss Adair beyond reach of danger? That is her father's house on the hill;" he pointed as he spoke to a mansion within view; "and she ought not to remain here, as we will be fighting at this spot in five minutes."

"I am not afraid," said the young lady in a perfectly composed voice.

"I beg Miss Adair will accede to my request," said Landon, coolly; "and that you, colonel, will oblige me. You can rejoin me at Millwood. I do not mean to make any stand here. My object is accomplished, and I am going to fall back, whether driven or not."

With these words Landon bowed to the young lady, and, clearing the fence, galloped up the hill.

Suddenly Arden met him, falling back rapidly. The crest of the hill swarmed with blue cavalry, firing quick volleys, and uttering loud cheers as the rangers doggedly gave ground. There was nothing for me to do but to conduct the young lady from the dangerous spot, or simply join in the retreat, and I chose the former. Throwing my cape over my horse, behind the saddle, I mounted, assisted her to her seat, and we galloped off in the midst of a shower of bullets, hissing like winged serpents around us.*

"Are you afraid?" I said.

"Not at all, sir."

And the speaker plainly was not.

We leaped a low fence, passed across a field, and ascended at full gallop a slope beyond.

* A fact.

From this elevated position I saw all. Landon's men were giving back step by step before enormous odds. The ground around the Old Chapel was full of clashing sabres, trampling hoofs, and quick shots flashing like fireflies against the dark foliage of the willows.

Then suddenly, as it were by enchantment, the swords ceased to clash, the hoofs to trample, and the shots to resound. All I heard was an occasional shout, and the stifled hum of a large force of Federal cavalry, drawn up in a long, dark column on the slope of the hill beyond the Chapel.

Landon and his Night-Hawks had vanished like phantoms in the darkness.

XI.

My situation was now peculiar.

The hour of the night was advanced; I was in a country nearly unknown to me, and swarming with the blue people; Landon and his Rangers had disappeared, and, to complicate the whole affair, I had under my charge a young lady, for whose safety I felt responsible.

It is possible that some readers of these pages will suppose that the tableau here presented of the cavalier, with his fair burden *en croupe,* is the result of imagination. I assure them that such is not the fact. The late war was a veritable repetition of the scenes of romance, and I assure the reader that I actually thus heroically "carried off" a very beautiful girl, with the bullets whistling around us; that her hand actually rested upon my shoulder; that her ringlets, when I turned my head, nearly brushed my cheek; and that, when I asked if she was afraid, she replied with extreme calmness in the manner above related.

To continue my narrative, Miss Adair scarcely

5   65

spoke during the whole ride, which was rapid, however, and soon came to an end.

She seemed to labour under some painful emotion; and I knew afterwards that this resulted from her brief interview with Landon. We went on thus in profound silence almost, and soon approached the large mansion indicated by Landon.

It raised its walls amid deep foliage on a lofty hill, and it was plain that the house and grounds had once been models of elegance. Now all was changed. The fences had been torn down; the boughs of the ornamental trees were broken and champed by cavalry horses, which had also trampled the fine turf, and the house looked bare and melancholy. It was a specimen of the houses and grounds of the entire Shenandoah Valley. Generals Hunter and Sheridan had not been able to conquer, — they had destroyed. What one left, the other took. When they retired, this Arcadia was a desert; the beautiful valley a Vale of Jehoshaphat.

Miss Adair dismounted and begged me to enter. I hesitated, but, after reflecting an instant, accepted the invitation; impelled, I am afraid, by two ignoble sentiments, — curiosity and — hunger!

I am trying to paint truly the "men and manners" of the late war, my dear reader; and marching and fighting made us terribly hungry!

It was plain that the good house had not lost the

old traditions of hospitality. A servant boy, — one of the few left, I fancy, — ran and took my horse to the stable; and then Miss Adair ushered me into a large drawing-room, illumined only by the moon.

As I entered, I heard a voice from the apartment opposite call out : —

" Is that you, my child? "

" Yes, father," was the reply.

And the young lady hastened thither, having first placed a lighted lamp upon the centre-table of the drawing-room.

The apartment had been elegant, but now looked "torn down." At one end was a bow-window, the recess half concealed by falling curtains.

I was gazing around me still, when the young lady came back and said : —

" Papa will be glad to see you, Colonel Surry. He is an invalid and cannot come out. Will you go in and see him? "

I bowed, and, following Miss Adair, entered the chamber where a gentleman of about sixty, with long gray hair, sparkling eyes, and a thin face, " thorough-bred," and full of character, lay upon a sofa.

He received me with old school courtesy, and Miss Adair having hastened out to prepare supper, I conversed for ten minutes with my host, Judge Adair, of the Supreme Court of Virginia.

If the readers of this page have seen my *Memoirs*, they will remember, perchance, the brief sketch therein of Colonel Beverley of "The Oaks,"—that ardent follower of Calhoun, and veritable firebrand of revolution. Well, my dear reader, Judge Adair rather surpassed the colonel. Need I say more? I had heard bitter denunciation of the North, listened to ferocious diatribes upon the doings of the blue people, but they were all milk and water, sugar and honey, compared with the observations of Judge Adair on that night of 1864!

For the rest I was not astonished. Will any one be? He lived in that region which a hostile fate seemed to have surrendered to the furies. Outrage, insult, and plunder had driven him to a species of scornful frenzy.

Never shall I forget that spectacle. Prostrated by sickness, unable almost to raise his head, the old lion glared with his fiery eye; lamenting most, it seemed, the weakness which kept his hand from the sword.

I will not repeat our conversation. My narrative deals with events. In the midst of it, Miss Adair came in and informed me that supper was ready, and I arose and followed her into the drawing-room, where an excellent repast awaited me.

I had scarce approached the table, however, when my fair young hostess laid her hand upon my arm.

I looked at her.   Her head was turned over her shoulder, and she was listening attentively.

Suddenly the origin of this movement was made plain to me.   The quick tramp of hoofs was distinguishable on the turf without; the ring of a sabre, as a cavalier dismounted; and rapid steps were heard ascending the steps which led to the front door of the mansion.

"Good heavens!" exclaimed Miss Adair, "they are Yankees, and you will be captured!   Come with me, Colonel Surry!"— and she almost dragged me toward the recess, concealed by the curtains, — "there is no time to, — here they are!"

I ignobly retreated behind the curtain, and at the same moment a man entered the apartment.

XII.

CAPTAIN RATCLIFFE.

In the new-comer I recognized the officer whom Landon had attacked and defeated near Millwood — Captain Ratcliffe, U.S.A.

He was about twenty-six, tall, imposing, and exceedingly handsome. A magnificent beard and moustache covered half of his face; his eyes were large and brilliant; and his splendid blue uniform set off the powerful figure to very great advantage. Captain Ratcliffe was evidently proud of his person, and, if he had left his sword and pistols behind, might have passed for a military beau on a visit.

But he came fully armed, and the sound of voices and horses' hoofs on the lawn without indicated that he had not come alone.

From my hiding-place I witnessed what followed.

The young lady remained quiet and did not respond to the bow of the officer.

"Good-evening, Miss Adair," he said; "my visit does not seem to be agreeable to you."

The young lady did not reply.

" You doubtless regard me as an intruder ? "

No response.

" Ah ! my uniform is hateful to you; or is it *I*, madam, that enjoy that privilege ? "

A growl accompanied the words. Captain Ratcliffe was evidently losing his temper rapidly.

" Speak, I beg, madam ! " he exclaimed, " unless you are dumb, or you think me unworthy of your ladyship's notice ! "

Miss Adair's eye flashed at the scornful tone of the speaker.

" I do not reply to you," she said, " because this visit is an intrusion, sir ! If I was not alone and helpless here, you would not come and force your presence upon me ! "

Ratcliffe flashed a dark look at her. Then, with a sarcastic laugh, he said : —

" I have only dropped in to enjoy the smiles of Venus after the frowns of Mars, madam. We have had a little affair to-night down yonder at the Chapel, — and by the by, we defeated and put to flight your dear friend Landon, of the Night-Hawks. He had the imprudence to attack us with about two hundred men; we had only about a hundred; and in half an hour we had the valiant jayhawker running."

" I was near," said Miss Adair, with extreme scorn in her voice, " and saw all."

" You ! " exclaimed the Federal captain.

" Yes, at the Chapel, sir, and I witnessed the whole engagement which you speak of. Captain Landon had about twenty-five men; your picket alone was double that number; he drove your picket, defeated you, and did not retire until you brought up a regiment or a brigade ! "

The calm voice, full of pride and defiance, made Ratcliffe flush with rage.

" Then we are babies ! cowards ! " he exclaimed, "and your friend is a hero ! "

In the intonation of these words, I recognized a hatred toward Landon as profound as his own for Ratcliffe.

" I am a coward ! afraid of him ! Come, acknowledge, madam, that you regard me as a poltroon ! "

She glanced through the window.

" Do you always go guarded in visiting ladies, sir ? " she said, quietly.

Ratcliffe started with rage.

" Curse the guard ! " he exclaimed, rudely. " I can take care of myself."

The young lady's lip moved slightly.

" And yet you Federal gentlemen always come attended thus, sir."

Ratcliffe scowled at the speaker, and said : —

" Do you think I am afraid ? "

"You are the best judge of that, sir," was the young lady's reply.

Ratcliffe uttered a species of growl, and, turning abruptly, called : —

"Orderly!"

A boy of eighteen appeared at the door and saluted. He was elegantly clad, and his countenance was one of extraordinary beauty.

"Order the men to retire to camp!" exclaimed Ratcliffe.

The boy saluted, but stood still, his eyes fixed upon Miss Adair. A strange expression had come to them; they seemed to blaze.

"What are you staying for?" growled the officer.

"Shall I go too?" said the boy in a voice full of music.

"You? — certainly!"

"I thought as I was your orderly, Captain —"

He paused; they exchanged a glance; and Ratcliffe said : —

"Well, remain; but send the company back to camp."

The boy disappeared, and in five minutes I heard the tramp of hoofs, which gradually receded and died away.

Then the young orderly again made his appearance, and said in the same musical voice : —

"The men are gone, captain."

As he spoke, I observed again the strange expression of his eyes, as he gazed at Miss Adair.

"Good!" said Ratcliffe; "wait outside."

And he made an imperious gesture. In spite of it the boy lingered, and it was only when Ratcliffe directed toward him a look full of menace that he sullenly obeyed.

The officer turned to Miss Adair.

"I am alone now, madam," he said, frowning.

"With a young girl only," she replied.

"A young girl and a gentleman!"

I laid my hand upon my pistol.

"Your beloved Landon," Ratcliffe sneered, "and his jayhawkers — the cowardly scoundrels! — may be away; but where is your father?"

"Here!" a voice said.

And, limping forward on his crutch, the old cavalier, with fiery eyes, and gray hair streaming over his shoulders, entered the apartment.

He advanced straight toward Ratcliffe, who gazed at him sullenly.

"Call St. Leger Landon a coward in my presence again!" exclaimed the old gentleman, "and I will cram the words down your dastardly throat!"

Ratcliffe recoiled, and made a movement to draw his pistol.

Before he could grasp it, I reached his side at one

bound, placed my own weapon close to his breast, and ordered : —

" Surrender, or you are dead ! "

Never shall I forget the expression of his countenance, the sudden pallor, the profound surprise, and his unnerved look, as he staggered back.

" Unbuckle your belt," I said.

He ground his teeth and obeyed.

" Throw your arms on that floor."

Without a word he threw down sabre and pistol, and they fell with a clatter upon the carpet at his feet.

Suddenly, as the sound echoed through the house, the young orderly appeared at the door.

" Surrender ! " I said, pointing my pistol at his head.

His reply was a military one. He drew his pistol and fired at me. I returned the shot with equal non-success ; and, seeing that he had missed me, the orderly disappeared at one bound, leaped on his horse, and vanished in the darkness.

There was now but one course left me, — to get away before the arrival of the men to whom the orderly would give the alarm. I intended, for the rest, to have Captain Ratcliffe for a travelling companion, and I found little difficulty in persuading him of the prudence of obeying.

My horse was quickly brought. I directed Ratcliffe to mount; and, saluting Judge Adair and his daughter, set out rapidly on the White Post road.

I held Ratcliffe's bridle in my left hand; with the right I directed a pistol at his breast.

He made no sort of resistance, and we went on at full speed through the moonlight.

XIII.

A MOONLIGHT RIDE.

IT was a singular ride.

For half a mile not a word was exchanged; the soft road deadened the sound of the horses' hoofs; animals and riders might have been taken, in the weird moonlight, for phantoms.

I continued to direct my pistol at Ratcliffe's breast, and to hold the bridle of his horse.

Going on thus rapidly, we crossed a little stream and entered a forest, through which the moonlight scarcely penetrated sufficiently to indicate the road.

All at once it occurred to me that we might run into a Federal picket, and I said : —

" Is there a picket near here, Captain Ratcliffe ? "

He made no reply.

" I ask you if there is a picket in these woods ? "

He preserved the same sullen silence, and I began to lose my temper.

Leaning over, and placing the muzzle of my pistol close to his head, I said : —

" You will reply to my question ! "

" There is no picket anywhere here," he growled.

"Good!" I said. "It seems to me you might have given a civil answer to a civil question at first, sir."

All at once I saw him turn his head and listen; I imitated the worthy, and heard distinctly the sound of hoofs coming on behind us, — the horses evidently at a headlong gallop.

I could see Ratcliffe's face flush in the moonlight, and an instant afterward he attempted a ruse to escape.

We were passing at full speed over the narrow woodland road, and had much difficulty in avoiding the trees. As we approached one nearly in the middle of the road, I felt Ratcliffe gradually oblique his horse to the left, and all at once the aim of this manœuvre became apparent. If he could pass just to the left of the tree, while I passed to the right, I would necessarily be compelled to release my hold upon his bridle, and then, by suddenly wheeling his horse, he might escape.

Unfortunately for him, I divined his intention. I allowed him to oblique more and more to the left, — the tree was now within a few feet of us, and the animals were about to pass to the right and left of it, — when I suddenly drew Ratcliffe's bridle violently toward me, and passed *with him* close to the tree, and on the right of it.

The consequence was that his knee struck the

trunk, his boot was nearly torn from his leg, and he uttered a deep groan.

"Another attempt of that sort and you are dead!" I said.

"You would fire on an unarmed prisoner, then?" he muttered.

"Attempting escape? yes. Try it, try it, my dear Captain Ratcliffe! Your friends yonder are gaining on us."

He turned his head and the flush of hope deepened. That made the blood mount to my own brain.

"They are coming! they may recapture you. I would much rather have them recapture your dead body."

But bad fortune was in store for me. As I spoke, my horse ran in the darkness against a sharp granite ledge cropping out from the bank, staggered, and, going ten paces, reeled and fell with me.

As he did so, I heard a loud cheer behind, and the pursuing party came on like a thunder-gust.

I rose quickly from my struggling horse. I had never released my clutch on Ratcliffe's bridle.

"Dismount!" I shouted, putting my pistol to his breast, "or —"

He did not let me finish. In half a second he had thrown himself from the saddle, and I vaulted into his place just as the pursuers rushed on, shout-

ing and firing.   I did not tarry.   Burying the spur
in Ratcliffe's horse, which was an excellent animal,
I went on at full speed; heard the men behind me
draw rein a few moments, and shout to Ratcliffe;
then they came on again upon my track.

But the delay had saved me.   Arrested by the
fallen horse in the middle of the road, the party had
stopped for two or three minutes: those minutes I
had utilized to their utmost.   I now turned into a
woodland path on the right, which I followed at the
utmost speed of my horse, and then I had the great
satisfaction of hearing the Federal cavalry rush by
on the road which I had left.

Their prey had escaped.

XIV.

Such had been the result of my ride with Landon to the Old Chapel. I had witnessed an animated skirmish; been present at a night burial of the dead; made the acquaintance under peculiar circumstances of a very charming young lady; captured a Federal officer; narrowly escaped capture myself; and was lost in the woods.

That was enough of adventure for one night, — was it not, reader? I thought so; and all I now asked of the kind fates was a monotonous and humdrum termination of this "series of events," — permission simply to lie down with my blanket around me, and sleep tranquilly, with "none to make me afraid."

Man proposes only. This night was not to pass away without something more to remember.

I was now in the midst of the woods, not far from the Federal lines, and the bridle path which I followed might lead me straight into a "Yankee picket." I went on, however, keeping a good lookout; and at last reached a road which I at once

6   81

recognized as the Old County Road, from Millwood to Winchester.

I had scarcely debouched from the forest, when a horseman, lost in the shadow of a great oak, called out suddenly : —

"Halt!"

The click of a pistol followed.

"Who goes there?" said the voice.

"Your comrade, lieutenant," I replied, for I had recognized the voice of Arden. And I rode to meet him.

"Colonel Surry?"

"In person, my dear Arden."

And I gave him an account of my adventures. The youth laughed heartily, congratulated me on my escape, and then said : —

"Well, Landon is beyond Millwood in bivouac, and I am going on a little scout."

I thought I saw the youth blush in the moonlight as he spoke.

"Ah! a scout," I said, laughing, as we rode on toward Winchester.

"To see a friend — "

And Arden certainly blushed this time.

"Good!" I cried. "I think I know the name of your friend, my dear Arden."

"Impossible!"

"Her name is Miss Annie."

" What an idea, colonel ! "

But the laugh of boyish pleasure revealed all.

" My guess is a natural one."

" Natural ? "

> " ' And Annie — I ask myself all the day long,
> If Annie is thinking of me,' "

was my reply, with a smile.

Arden blushed and again laughed.

" Don't think I make fun of you," I said; " by
no means, my dear Arden. It is good to love, and,
although our acquaintance is short, I take a very
sincere interest in you. I have seen you fighting,
and in bivouac too, and I would like to call you
friend, if you will let me."

The words evidently won his heart.

" I am proud to think you wish to," he said, with
boyish candor and earnestness; " and now I will
not conceal anything from you, colonel. You
laugh; but you do not seem to laugh *at* people."

Acknowledge, reader, that the compliment was
charming.

" Then it is really Miss Annie you are going to
see ? "

" Yes, colonel."

" Your cousin, or playmate in childhood, doubtless? "

" Oh! no; I am not of this country."

"You are not a Virginian?"

"I am a Yankee," said Arden, smiling; "that is to say, I was born in Delaware."

"And came to Virginia to help us?"

"Not exactly, colonel. I will tell you my history in a very few words, if you wish to hear it."

"I should like much to."

"Well, to begin at the beginning. I will not be tedious, and this splendid moonlight night makes one feel like talking. The Ardens have lived for nearly two hundred years in Delaware, and my father was for a quarter of a century one of the State officers of that Commonwealth. Wealthy by inheritance, he became poor, like many other gentlemen, by profuse hospitality; and his two sons — Ralph and myself — saw that it was our duty to endeavour to become producers instead of consumers. Well, Ralph, who was impetuous and full of energy, chose arms for his profession, and at seventeen secured a place at West Point, leaving me at home. I was of exactly the same age, — as Ralph and myself were twins, — and it made me so ashamed to remain at home, that one day I went to my father, and said, 'I wish you would let me go into a merchant's counting-house, and earn my bread, sir.' But my father shook his head. 'I intend you for the law, my son, and trade will spoil you,' he said. 'Then I must go somewhere and teach,' I replied; 'I can do so, and study too.' To this, my father consented, and, seeing the advertisement of a gentleman in the Valley here, whom he knew, my father wrote to him and secured the place of teacher in his family for me. A week afterwards I was in Virginia, teaching the young idea how to shoot."

"The name of one of the 'young ideas,'" I said, laughing, "being Miss Annie."

Arden smiled, and shook his head.

"You are wrong, colonel. Of course, however, one thing brought on the other. My visit to Virginia made me acquainted with — her."

Arden blushed a little as he pronounced the word "her," pausing before it.

"She lived only a mile off," he continued, "at an old house called 'The Briars,' whither we are now going. Her aunt, with whom she lived, was not the owner of the estate. The family to whom it belonged had moved from it, and Mrs. Meadows — that was her name — was the tenant; a most excellent lady, as you will have an opportunity of seeing, I hope, to-night."

"Well," I said, with a smile, seeing Arden pause.

He looked at me, blushing a little, with "What more?" plainly written in his face.

I began to laugh.

"My dear Arden," I said, "this is only the

preface. Tell me of your little affair! I am
anxious, I assure you; for nothing could be more
'dramatic' in a quiet, pastoral, idylic way, than
your history. Observe the 'situation,' as we say in
the army. You are a young gentleman of the
North, and ought, by rights, to be courting some
little *blue* belle of New England, or other portions
of that favoured land, and in the *blue* army. Instead of which, see what the real fact is! You are
enamoured of a little lily of the Virginia Valley,
and an officer in the *gray* forces. Finish, finish!
my dear Arden."

"I see that nothing will satisfy you, colonel," he
said, shyly, "but the whole explanation."

"You are right."

"Well, I soon became a friend of the family and
a regular visitor; and when the war broke out went
into the Confederate army. I beg you not to think,
however, that I yielded to somebody's solicitations,
and joined the South against my principles. No,
indeed, colonel! You would do me very great injustice in thinking so. My whole family are anti-
war democrats, and I was raised in the strictest
State-rights doctrines from my childhood. 'The
States are sovereign,' my father had said to us a
hundred times; and when South Carolina seceded
in the winter of 1860, he wrote to me, 'I deplore it;
but peaceable secession is the corner-stone of State

rights.' So you see, I did not sell my sword for a young lady's smile! I was too proud to do that; I should have thought it a dishonour; and I would not dishonour myself, colonel, for any consideration in this world! I said to myself — for *she* did not open her lips to me — I said 'This government is either an empire, and the States are provinces, or it is a league of *sovereignties* who have parted with a few clearly defined rights only, reserving the rest. If it is an empire, secession is rebellion against legally constituted authority, and calls for suppression and punishment; as a rebellion in Yorkshire would be suppressed and punished. If the government, on the contrary, is a league of sovereign commonwealths, then secession is the exercise of a *right*, and to oppose it is a *wrong;* to make war, for that reason, and force the South back into a hateful union, is open tyranny, — the stronger oppressing the weaker.' Well, when I reached that point, in my train of reasoning, I said to myself, 'What is your duty? — to aid the oppressor or the oppressed? — to offer your sword to the stronger, or the weaker side?' And that question did not long puzzle me."

I extended my hand and grasped Arden's.

"It was the decision of a brave gentleman, and I honour you," I said.

"Then you believe me?" said the young man, laughing and sighing.

" Believe you ! — "

" Many do not. They say, yonder in Delaware, I am told, that a young lady has 'demoralized' me ; the war people say it, not my father."

" Let them say it."

Arden's head rose proudly.

" You are right, colonel. There is nothing like doing your duty. I am trying to do mine, and I appeal to God for the sincerity of my convictions in this war. I did not hesitate a moment. At the first sound of the trumpet I entered the Confederate ranks as a private. I was young, untrained, but tried to do my duty. I am not much, — a mere boy; but Captain Landon is my friend, and by his partiality I have become a lieutenant, — by that only."

" I do not believe a word of that ! I have seen you at the broadsword exercise," I said, laughing ; " and your brother ? "

" He is in the United States Army."

" You have seen him ? "

" More than once, but — God be thanked ! — never crossed swords with him yet."

" He is in the cavalry ? "

" Yes, and what is still more, in Ratcliffe's company — a lieutenant."

" That is bad, indeed," I said, thinking of my own brother Will, in the Northern army.

"Very bad."

"You love each other?"

"With all our hearts, colonel. Oh, you should know Ralph, if you admire real courage, and heart, and honour! He is the coolest, bravest, noblest fellow that ever lived."

"Pity he is not with us."

Arden shook his head.

"Ralph thinks we are a set of outrageous rebels, and would rather die than change his colours.

"He is right."

"Yes; but we have made a bargain."

"A bargain?"

"Not to kill each other if possible!" said Arden, laughing.

And suddenly extending his hand toward a mansion buried in trees, and in sight of the road: —

"That is her house," he said, blushing like a boy.

"Her" house! That told the whole story.

XV.

ARDEN had unconsciously touched his horse with the spur, as he spoke, and we cantered over the rough and unused road toward the mansion which he had pointed out.

"That is 'The Briars,' probably," I said.

"Yes, colonel, one of many old mansions you have seen or passed to-day, — 'Chapeldale,' 'Newmarket,' 'The Meadow,' 'Pagebrooke,'" — where something of old times still lingers, Heaven be thanked! and will linger, I trust, to the end of the chapter; or, during my time, at least!"

"Fie, Arden! You are an aristocrat, a believer in the past!"

"A very devout believer," said the young man, joyously. "You uphold *class*, — don't you, colonel?"

"No, I'm a leveller."

"You? Good heavens!"

"You doubt my sincerity?"

"Completely, I am sorry to say, colonel."

"Well, you are wrong, my dear Arden. I think

that whatever is, is best; and is not everybody equal to everybody else? Consult the immortal Jefferson!"

"I wish he had never lived."

"Fie! you think with his opponent, Randolph of Roanoke."

Arden's face glowed.

"Indeed I do, my dear colonel. If there ever was a wise statesman it was your Randolph of Roanoke. People called him erratic, crack-brained, unreliable. But I'll tell you what I think: I think he was the profoundest and wisest political thinker this country ever produced."

I began to laugh.

"Well," I said, "let us not further discuss these high themes. I very much fear that you are still in the gall of bitterness and the bonds of iniquity, my young friend. My own opinion is, that everybody, high and low, black and white, good and bad, educated and ignorant, is equal to everybody else. Now, as this is not very interesting, let us come back to your little affair."

"There's no time, colonel. Here is 'The Briars.' Follow me through this gate in the stone fence, and we'll go round to the front of the house."

As Arden spoke, he leaped his horse through the torn-down wall; I followed, and, skirting a piece of water at the lower end of a grove, we entered a meadow, and saw the house to our right. It was a stone building, stuccoed, of considerable size, and with a long portico in front, overshadowed by trees. Across the rolling fields in front was seen the long wave of the North Mountain, like a faint mist on the horizon. Toward the south a body of woods arrested the view.

"Ah, here is the picture that an invisible artist used to paint for you 'in your tent on the Rapidan,' Arden!" I said. "Where's the 'oriole that sang in the sycamore-tree?' I suspect the name of the oriole was *Annie*, — was it not?"

"You are a terrible tease, colonel," said the blushing Arden; "and if you laugh at me any more, I will ask after the health of the 'Rose of Fauquier,' whose other name is Miss May Beverley."

The shot dismounted me. From the aged philosopher and satirist, I found myself reduced suddenly to the character of a romantic lover, — no better than Harry Arden.

"Well aimed, my boy," I said; "and I'm silenced. Let us drop the subject and get on."

"We have arrived, colonel!" And Arden threw open the gate.

All at once, as he did so, we heard the trample of hoofs behind the house.

Then a squad of gray-clad horsemen appeared dashing toward the stable on the left of the house, shouting "Halt! Halt!"

XVI.

WE entered the grounds, and spurred after the gray figures. Suddenly we found our course arrested by a high plank fence; and, forced thus to check our horses, witnessed a singular scene, without taking any part in it.

The Confederates were pressing hotly a young Federal officer, whose blue uniform was perfectly plain in the bright moonlight.

He had issued from the house, and, running to the stable, called to a terrified orderly, who stood fumbling at the bridle, to bring him his horse. The orderly seemed wholly incapable of obeying; and uttering a loud shout, the Confederates, entering by an open gate, rode straight at the officer.

As they did so, the young man wheeled round and confronted them, drawing his pistol, and coolly cocking it, without the least exhibition of alarm.

There was something superb in his bearing, and I exclaimed : —

"That is a brave fellow!"

"Good heavens!" I heard Arden say; "it is my brother Ralph!"

" Is it possible ? "

" Yes."

The Confederates were now nearly upon him.

" Halt ! "

" Surrender ! "

And the men drew their pistols as they spoke.

" Never with life ! " * I heard the young officer reply in a clear, collected voice.

And, raising his pistol, he took deliberate aim ; the discharge followed, and the foremost Confederate fell from his horse, shot through the neck and mortally wounded.

As the animal wheeled and ran, the young officer coolly uttered the monosyllable : —

" One ! "

The second confederate fired at him within six paces, but missed.   The report of the Federal officer's pistol followed it like an echo, and the second Confederate, throwing up his arms, fell from the saddle like the first.

" Two ! " came in the same deep tone.

By this time the whole party had rushed into the stable-yard.   I glanced at Arden beside me.   He was as pale as death.

" They will butcher him ! " he muttered.

" Wait ! " I said ; " I am not so sure of that."

In fact, the result seemed extremely doubtful.

* His words.

The young Federal officer was plainly not at all "demoralized." Instead of retreating into the stable, he advanced full into the open space lit by the moon, and I could see that his belt was full of pistols.

Then I witnessed a superb spectacle. Not without reason had Arden called his brother "cool" and "brave." I had seen exhibitions of "game" often during the war; but a cooler man than the young Federal officer, never.

He advanced straight upon his opponents, took dead aim, fired shot after shot, and every shot appeared to wound or bring down a man. In the midst of a shower of bullets, he seemed to possess a charmed life; none struck him. And still came that deadly echo from his own weapon! The words "three! four!" accompanied by the fall of the men at whom he fired, testified to the fatal accuracy of his aim.

This lasted at least ten minutes ; at the end of that time Lieutenant Arden, U. S. A., was master of the field.

I saw him coolly replace his empty pistol in its holster, catch the bridle of a horse belonging to one of the Confederates whom he had shot, and then turn to the frightened orderly.

"Orderly!" he said, in a perfectly calm voice.

" Lieutenant ! " came in a trembling voice from the stable.

" What a coward you are ! " said the other, laughing.

A sort of moan replied.

" Come out, you rascal ! "

The trembling orderly appeared.

" Mount; lead my horse and come, or rather go on."

The victim of fright obeyed, and was soon galloping off.

" Now, for number five ! " said the officer, smiling satirically ; " they fire badly, these gentlemen."

And, advancing coolly toward his adversaries, who were crowded together in a little lane, waiting for him to mount, he took deliberate aim at them, fired, and looked to see if his shot had struck. Then, as calmly as before, he again took aim, and again fired.

These two parting shots exhausted, it seemed, his loads. The young officer replaced his pistol in his belt, threw himself on the horse of the wounded cavalryman, which he had continued to hold by the bridle, and, waving his hat around his head, galloped off. *

In a minute he had disappeared, hotly pursued by

* Fact.

the cavalrymen, who, recoiling before his deadly aim while on foot, waited for him to mount, in order to follow on his track. They did so, now, at full speed, and I heard shots resound; then they died away, and all vanished.

Arden drew a long breath.

" Good heavens! what a man!" he exclaimed.

" What a brave man!"

" My brother?"

" Yes. I could have killed him by a bullet through the side or back. Do you think I would have fired on him? I would rather have cut off my right hand."

" Thanks, colonel," said the young man. And, with a quick blush, he added: —

" Here is Annie!"

In fact, a young girl came out with a light, and I saw a rosy little face, framed in curls, shine in the circle of radiance. Arden threw himself from horseback, introduced his friend Colonel Surry to Miss Annie Meadows; and an old lady, with thin, gray hair under a white cap, having made her appearance, the wounded cavalrymen were borne, with the assistance of a maid-servant, into the house, and their wants cared for.

Half an hour afterwards the wounded men were dozing on couches spread on the floor of the apartment, or occupied beds elsewhere; and Miss Annie

7

and Arden were whispering in a corner by the light
of a glimmering candle.

It was a charming picture. The young faces
glowed, the lips smiled, and the eyes were full of an
expression which the present writer carefully guards
himself from "making fun of." I knew afterwards
that the young lady was explaining the visit of Arden's brother, — an explanation which the reader
will have laid before him in due season; and I
suppose the "young things" talked of various other
subjects.

I can see them now, sitting in their little nook
by the window, bending toward each other, looking
into each other's eyes, smiling, blushing, — and —
yes! as I live, "shaking hands." Enough of this
improper espial. Whisper, fond young lovers in the
moonlight night. Press hands, murmur low, enjoy
your chance meeting on the border. Be absurd, be
foolish, be as much "in love" as you choose. Some
cynics may laugh at you, but among them will not
be the smiling Colonel Surry, who listened for a
few moments to the prattle of the lovers, and then
snored in his rocking-chair.

At daylight I awoke and aroused Arden, who was
sleeping in a chair beside me. Miss Annie had disappeared.

Fifteen minutes afterwards we were mounted and
had regained the main road. A glance around told

me that I was near the Opequon, and consequently a few miles only from Winchester, whither duty called me.

"Good-by," I said, after having informed Arden of the latter fact. "I will see you soon again, I hope, and make you sing for me of Annie!"

"You laugh, colonel, but it is a good-natured laugh. Isn't she worth it?"

"Indeed she is."

"Come again and see us soon."

"Without fail!" And we parted with a close grasp of the hand.

Two hours afterwards I had forded the Opequon, passed Early's picket on the crest of hills over-looking Winchester, and the paving-stones of that ancient border town resounded beneath my horse's feet.

That horse was Ratcliffe's splendid charger, from which I had made him dismount. It was the sole memorial which I retained of those two nights of adventure on the banks of the Shenandoah.

XVII.

WINCHESTER.

I WONDER if these memories interest you, friendly reader, as much as they interest the person who records them?

Pursuing thus the path of my recollections and my dreams, I go back to the past, which amuses me much more than the present, and its figures live and move for me again as they once did in the flesh!

1864, with all its drawbacks, was exciting, at least. 1868 is so dull! — is it not, reader?

I think so; and try to make the shadow run back on the dial. Instead of talking about reconstruction which does not reconstruct, and that republican liberty supported so gracefully on bayonets, I return to 1864, and tell my story of the border.

Again the carbines ring and the sabres clash. Good carbines! trusty sabres! — one hangs on my wall yonder, — you are useless now, and are rusting wofully! but I try to make your echoes sound again as in the hours of old. The present epoch is stupid, — why not try to enliven it? So I ponder here at *Eagle's Nest;* and, falling into dreams as it were, see the past return. All comes back to memory, fresh and living, — the days and nights of adventure, the charging squadrons, the ringing shouts; all the romance and incident, — the mingled comedy and tragedy of "that place and time," — the border in 1864.

That word "romance" was injudicious. I am not writing romance. Do you doubt that assertion? Perhaps, you say, for example, that the incident just related — that courageous conduct of the young Federal officer — is imaginary. It is true in every detail; and for the accuracy of other incidents ask the old followers of Mosby, and Gilmore, and O'Neil. I only fear that my picture is too tame.

My narrative lags, and yet I am greatly tempted to tarry a little in the good old town of Winchester, to say a few words of the place and some famous personages whom I encountered there, in this September of 1864.

Perhaps you imagine that Winchester is too small to deserve much attention, reader. Never was greater mistake; and that philosophy, too, is errour. *Size* is not the measure of *importance* in countries, cities, or men. Greece was only a spot on the map of the Old World; and yet she fertilized all countries with her ideas. Macedon was small; but her king conquered Persia, — the greatest empire of the earth.

Prussia was small; but she held her own against Europe in arms.

Among cities is Paris or Pekin the most notable? One moves in advance of the world; the other is dragged, a huge bulk, unwieldy and shapeless, as limitless, inert Asia is dragged by little Europe.

And as to men: size is less a measure of importance there than elsewhere. Napoleon was the "Little Corporal." Vendome was a microscopic hunchback. Pope was a dwarf.

Granite and marble are not more valuable than the ruby and the diamond, because the ruby and the diamond are less bulky.

And Winchester is not insignificant, because it is a place of only five or six thousand inhabitants.

All which reflections, my dear reader, have, it is true, no connection with our narrative, but, like the few pages following, have a distinct aim in view. I have just shown you a number of scenes of a very hurried and "dramatic" description, and we are going to rest a little now, and walk arm in arm through Winchester.

It is a queer old place, — is it not? These overturned stones are the ruins of Fort Loudoun, which a young man, called George Washington, just promoted to be major, but now forgotten, commanded against the French and Indians about one hundred years ago. Look at the old, gray-walled church yonder, surrounded by its crumbling tombstones. Under the shadow of its walls, lie General Daniel Morgan, the friend of Washington and victor of Tarleton ; and Lord Fairfax, former owner of all this portion of Virginia.

Morgan was brave among the brave, but there was no pretence about him.

" Old Morgan was often miserably afraid ! " he said.

And when coming to die he murmured : —

" To be only twenty again, I would be willing to be stripped naked, and hunted through the Blue Ridge with wild dogs ! "

Near him sleeps Lord Fairfax, who was the friend and patron of Washington in the latter's boyhood. Like Morgan, he died in Winchester here, and his last hours were bitter. It was in 1781. Yorktown had just fallen. Cornwallis had surrendered to Washington, and the people of Winchester raised a shout.

" What is that ? " asked the gray-haired nobleman.

They told him, and he uttered a groan.

" Take me to bed, John," he murmured to his old English body-servant ; " it is time for me to die ! "

And soon afterwards he expired. His bones were laid far from " Old England," the home of his race, in the quiet church-yard here, at Winchester, which he had built up.   All through the Indian wars the place had been a sentinel watching the border; and now it still watches Lord Fairfax's tomb.

A single additional historic incident.   At the old house yonder, about 1830, two travellers stopped, and, asking for dinner in their private apartment, were indignantly refused that request by the democratic landlord.

"If they thought they were too good to eat with the rest, they might leave the house."

The travellers bowed, and ordered their carriage, which then drove off elsewhere.   It contained Louis Philippe D'Orleans, afterwards King of the French, and his kinsman, the Duc de Montpensier.

Odd, original, crooked, suggestive old Winchester! But how friendly and cordial!   Yonder are the ruins of "Selma," the former residence of Senator Mason; and, all around you, are similar traces of Federal displeasure; but glimmering amid the ruins are cheerful faces and bright, sweet eyes.

They belong to the "women of Winchester," and that term is going to be as famous, one of these days, as "Roman Mother."

See those slender figures yonder, moving toward the hospitals!   They look fragile.   These girls are timid, you would say.   Do you think so?   When the enemy appear they wave Southern flags.   When the banner of the United States is suspended over the pavement they walk around it. When they pass Federal officers they draw their skirts aside, to prevent them from coming in contact with the blue uniforms. When Jackson drove Banks through the town, in 1862, details were obliged to go in advance to warn the girls out of the way, in order that the platoons might deliver their fire. After Kernstown they came out and ran to greet and cheer the Southern prisoners; and then, proceeding to the battle-field, sought out the Confederate corpses for burial. They bent over them, sobbing and weeping, so that a young Federal officer's heart ached at the sight.

"Do not cry so," he said to a young lady who seemed heart-broken.

The bowed head rose erect with intense hauteur, and the wet eyes blazed.

"What right have you to speak to me?" exclaimed the young lady, with burning indignation. "Why did your people invade our country? But you will never conquer us. We will never yield! We will shed the last drop of our blood before you shall trample on us!"

A place with such memories and such hearts is worth attention, — is it not?

For my own part, I never go to Winchester, without thinking, "Here is the true South! The hearts around me here were faithful in the dark days as in the bright. They were true, under all trials, to the bitter end; and, when others faltered, when others doubted, when brave men shrunk, and the most hopeful despaired, then Winchester was most resolved, — her resolution faltered least. Losing peace, competence, and suffering all woes, she still kept that irreproachable honour, of which nothing can ever deprive her, winning a clenched hand for crest, and for motto, ' True to the last! ' "

XVIII.

In this September, 1864, General Early was occupying Winchester. His little army, of eight or ten thousand, of all arms, was east of the town. General Sheridan's forces, consisting of thirty-five thousand infantry, and ten thousand cavalry, were lying on the right bank of the Opequon, a few miles distant.

So much in passing simply. The present memoir deals with the Partisans, not the "regular troops." At some other time I may describe that bitterly contested and long-doubtful battle of the Opequon, where Early held his ground all day, although outnumbered five to one. At present I do not touch the great canvas, contenting myself with rapid outlines of a few famous figures seen at Winchester then.

I found the brave General Early in his tent, near Winchester. Any one would have known him. The piercing eyes, the curling hair, the mordant smile, and stooping shoulders, could belong to no one but the fearless and obstinate fighter, called

familiarly by his men "Old Jube." Nicknames
indicate regard, when employed by troops. There
were some who disliked the general for his rigid dis-
cipline; but none were absurd enough to doubt his
courage.

"Old Jube aint afraid of the devil!" was the
rough saying in the army. Indeed, in the Army
of Northern Virginia there was no more resolute
soldier.

The general greeted me with a friendly smile, and
we had a long talk.

"Grant has been up to see his young friend,
'Cavalry Sheridan,'" he said, with that long-drawn
and deliberate intonation, amounting nearly to a
drawl, and smiling satirically as he spoke. "Grant
is a tremendous specimen of a soldier, and has given
Sheridan a tremendous order."

"What?"

"To 'go in;' that is, swallow a certain inoffensive
General Early!" And the speaker uttered a short
laugh, which I echoed.

At the same moment Colonel C—— entered, and
I exchanged with the brave artillerist a cordial
shake of the hand. The colonel then turned to
Early and said: —

"General, I have come to ask permission to go
down to *Annfield* to see my family for twenty-four
hours."

The general shook his head.

"Can't give you leave, colonel."

"But I have no horse, general, and can get one at home."

"Borrow one, colonel," retorted the general, with a humourous drawl. "I have been riding a borrowed horse through the whole campaign." *

It was impossible to avoid laughing at the tone of the speaker's voice; and Colonel C—— laughed too.

As he went out, General Rodes entered, followed by General Ramseur.

Did you meet, during the late war, those two heroic souls, reader? If not, let me draw a rapid outline of them; they deserve it. Among the braves who fell fighting in that terrible year 1864, none were braver, none more devoted, than the Virginian Rodes and the North Carolinian Ramseur.

Rodes — tall, slender, quiet, with blue eyes, long, light hair, light beard, and a smile as sweet as a woman's — impressed you slightly at first view. But a second glance revealed more. When he spoke, his voice was brief, resolute, quiet, but commanding. For the rest, your true soldier does not always *look like a soldier*. How many burly, black-bearded giants, with thunderous voices and boastings, have I seen falter! How many smooth-faced, girlish, low-

* His words.

voiced boys have I known who would fight to the
last and die unmoved! Willie Pegram, — shrinking
and shy, with the face and bearing of a girl, — how
you fought and fell, thrilling the whole Southern
army with that courage of the bull-dog!

Ramseur presented a strong contrast to his companion. Of medium height, dark-haired, with black
beard and eyes, animated, a real soldier in bearing,
you saw that he would lead a forlorn hope into the
muzzles of hostile cannon, and fight against any odds
to the last.

I spent an hour with the three generals, and then
took my leave. As I left Early's tent, I met one
who was building up then a great fame, — General
Gordon.

Gordon was a soldier born, — from head to foot,
soldier. The penetrating glance, the proud head
flanked by long hair carried behind the ears, the firm
lips, the resolute chin, the commanding carriage
of the whole person, showed that he was born for
leadership. His fame was a late-growing flower;
but how dazzling was the bloom when it came!
Have you ever seen the " Giant-of-battle " rose,
reader? — that superb, full disc, of flashing crimson,
which Stuart so loved? Here was the human
" giant of battle," — the man whose name was to
electrify the whole army, as it will electrify the
future; who, at Cedar Creek, the Wilderness, all

along the road to Petersburg, at Hare's Hill, and in the last charge at Appomattox, was to win a fame, shining clear, among the brightest in history.

I look back and remember meeting many great men; among them, few rise in stature to the level of Gordon. To receive his modest and cordial salute, with the friendly smile, charmed me; to press that hand, that held the sword-hilt with a grasp so heroic in battle, was a very great honour. I thought so then; I think so more than ever to-day.

Health and happiness attend you, general! You tread already on the shining heights of history. Three names to-day are greeted with a strange enthusiasm in the South. Those names are Lee, Hampton, and Gordon.

And now, looking back to that day at Winchester, I remember, with sighs, what the near hours brought.

Ramseur killed at the Opequon; Rodes killed at Cedar Creek; Early driven into exile, — how the strong hours crush us!

But these reflections are sad. Let us dismiss them and record more cheerful things.

I was invited on this evening to meet my friend, General Fitzhugh Lee, at Mr. M——'s; and, approaching the handsome portico flooded with moonlight, had a charming surprise.

Leaning on General Lee's arm was — Miss May Beverley!

XIX.

FITZHUGH LEE, THE GAY AND GALLANT.

"UNDER all the circumstances," I think I will say nothing more of Miss May Beverley.

Unfortunately, that young lady has already been brought too prominently before the world in the first series of my *Memoirs*, to which my friend, the editor, has given the title "Surry of Eagle's Nest."

If you have perused that volume, you must have felt some surprise, my dear reader, that a young damsel's private life and affairs of the heart should have been dwelt upon so unreservedly. But a word will explain all. My memoirs were written for my own family, and published only "by request of friends."

In sending off the MS., a pencil-mark was drawn through the obnoxious chapters. By some accident, however, they were printed, and Miss Beverley's affairs were made public. To-day, to avoid all further indiscretion, I preserve silence.

So, worthy reader, if you are curious about Miss May Beverley; if you wish to know how this star of loveliness and goodness (be still, madam, and don't

be so impolite as to look over my shoulder!) rose
above the horizon of my life; if you would find
where we met first; how I became a fortunate victim, — you have only to read the *Memoirs* to which
I refer.

In this place I will only say that mademoiselle
looked quite charming, and that the great violet
eyes and waving chestnut hair were brighter than
in the old days of 1861, at "The Oaks." She had
come to Winchester on a visit, and I had not seen
her at Colonel Beverley's. Her smile was sunshine,
her lips as red as carnations, and the rose in her
hair looked faded beside the two that bloomed in her
cheeks! (Are you satisfied, madam? That is
rather well-turned, I think! You see I have not
forgotten; that I remember you with the eyes as well
as the heart! I go away from *Eagle's Nest*, where
I write this with your face bending over me, in 1868,
to Winchester, in 1864, when you were far less
demonstrative! I see your smiles, hear your voice,
and listen! There is the gay laughter of the gallant General Fitz Lee, as he looks at me in triumph,
and bears you off, in the moonlight, with the white
hand on the gold braid of his gray coat-sleeve!)

I wish I had time and space to make a portrait of
that brave soldier and gentleman, Major-General
Fitzhugh Lee, or "General Fitz," as we used to
call him in the army. Never was born into this

world a gayer, more sparkling spirit, a truer comrade, a finer representative of the great race of
cavaliers. You had only to look at this dashing
sabreur, — the bosom-friend of Stuart, — at this
"cavalryman all over," with the soul of merriment,
truth, courage, frolic, resolution, and unwavering
"pluck," to see that he was born for the career of
arms, for the life of the bivouac and the battle-field.
As we pass, however hurriedly, let us glance at him
for an instant. Here he is, with his low and athletic
figure, his well-worn uniform, cavalry boots, gay
sash, and brown hat with its black feather. See the
flowing brown beard, and heavy mustache, like
Stuart's; the lips curling with laughter; the eyes
flashing with good-humour; hear the voice, rich and
mellow; note the bearing full of fun, and the *insou-
ciant* cavalry ease. A glance tells you that this
man is ready to mount at a moment's warning; that
the small white hand will go to the sword-hilt in-
stinctively, and that, wherever sabres clash, he will
be present.

You will find in many volumes, reader, an account of Fitzhugh Lee's performances : how he
fought through all the battles of Stuart; originated
the "Buckland-races" ruse; drove amain, with his
troopers, through the smoke of Manassas, Boonsboro',
Sharpsburg, Gettysburg; fought Sheridan in the
great campaigns of 1864, and on Lee's retreat, in

1865, commanded the rear guard of the army, fighting at every step, and made the last cavalry charge at Appomattox, ten minutes before the surrender. All this you will read, and you will find the testimony of his great kinsman, General R. E. Lee: "Your admirable conduct, devotion to the cause of your country, and devotion to duty, fill me with pleasure." Read all that in the books, friend. Here I show you not Major-General Fitzhugh Lee, fighting obstinately on desperate fields, but Fitz Lee, the gay and gallant, laughing as he bears off, with twinkling eyes, in the moonlight, the sweetheart (pardon that old word, reader!) of the unfortunate Colonel Surry.

I had recaptured the young lady, had my own little talk, and was laughing with my friend, "General Fitz," when a courier brought me a despatch. It was from General Lee's head-quarters, through General Early's, and directed me to make a thorough inspection of the entire Partisan forces of the region.

An hour afterwards, I had made all my preparations to obey this order, which would take me into the heart of "Mosby's Confederacy."

I had parted from Fitzhugh Lee with a warm pressure of the hand, little supposing that in a few days he would be prostrated by a dangerous wound, in a hot fight with Sheridan's cavalry. It laid him up for months, but he was again in the field in the spring, fighting as before. To the end he continued fighting, and he was the last to lay down his sword.

He is yonder to-day, at "Richland," on the Potomac, and an old comrade, from "Eagle's Nest," sends him greeting in the dull hours.

Health and happiness, "General Fitz!" May the breezes of the Chesapeake, which pass Richland, bear away the noise of laughter! Ten thousand hearts are beating in the South to-day which remember you. Ten thousand voices would repeat for you the words of our old army ballad,

"Here's my heart, and here's my hand,"

as does the comrade of old times, who writes this page.

XX.

THE order which I had received to make an inspection of the Partisan commands was far from disagreeable.

It enabled me to remain longer in the region than my original orders contemplated; and it thus seemed probable that I would witness the sequel of Landon's highly "dramatic" affair with Ratcliffe.

I really longed to be present, or not very far off, when the *denouement* of the tragedy took place; and I hope the reader will not, on that account, regard me as a very prying personage. He would do me injustice. I have always had a very profound respect for the individual — read of in romances — who made an ample fortune by attending to his own business. (And here let me exclaim, parenthetically, Oh, to make his acquaintance, if he be still alive! or to know, even, some member of his "small and select" family! Up to the present time, I have failed to enjoy the pleasure of their acquaintance!)

Not from prying curiosity, then, but from rational interest in a very curious drama, I had come to feel that desire to be near when Landon and Ratcliffe settled their differences. That the settlement would be bloody, there was little doubt. Between these two human beings there was evidently a bitter feud.

What was the origin of it? How would it terminate? What had been the relations between Miss Adair and Landon, and had not Ratcliffe played a part in the drama of these two lives? I had a decided longing to penetrate these mysteries; to ascertain what tie had bound my cool and resolute friend Landon to the young girl who had appeared so suddenly in the Old Chapel graveyard; to know all about him and Ratcliffe; to see what would be the *denouement* of all these loves, hatreds, and vengeances.

So I shook General Early's hand, and bade that hardy soldier farewell, to go back to the Partisans.

It was a beautiful morning in early September. The road which I followed was the main one to Millwood and Ashby's Gap; and, passing the Opequon, I pushed on, winding amid the hills, whose slopes were covered with the yellow and golden tints of the approaching autumn.

Leaving the "pine hills" as they are called, I advanced steadily, without encountering a single horseman, and had entered a forest within two or three miles of Millwood, when all at once I caught sight, through the tree-trunks, of a red flag, then of a column of mounted men drawn up at the mouth of a road debouching into the main highway.

A second glance told me that they were Landon's men, and I was soon at his side.

He greeted me, as did Arden, with a close pressure of the hand, and in a few words I explained what had happened after our parting at the Old Chapel.

"Good!" he said, "I am glad he got away from you, colonel."

"Ratcliffe?"

"Yes."

I laughed and said, "Is he a particular friend of yours?"

"Yes; and I think I am going to put my hand on him this morning, when I promise you he will not get away so easily."

Landon's voice was as cool and measured as ever, but there was an unwonted light in his eyes. It was the light in the eye of the bloodhound who sees his prey and longs to spring upon it.

"Ratcliffe is yonder," he continued, pointing across the woods to the right. "I have sent Touch-and-go to capture the *vidette,* so as to surprise him."

"What is his force?"

"About eighty.

"Your own?"

"About thirty."

"Look out!" I said, pointing to a figure in blue, hastening toward us; "they are coming to reconnoitre *you.*"

"It is Touch-and-go. Well?" he said, quickly, as the scout approached.

"Eighty-five men, captain. I counted them as they wound over the hill toward Saratoga."

"Good! and the vidette?"

"He is dead. He was at the gate in the stone fence. I walked straight up to him, thinking my blue coat would fool him; but he snapped his carbine at me."

"And —"

"I did not wish to shoot him, for fear of alarming them; so I got hold of his carbine and knocked out his brains with the butt-end."

"All right. Come on, colonel; we are losing time," said Landon.

And, placing himself at the head of his men, he went down the road toward Millwood at a thundering gallop.

Emerging from the woods, the Blue Ridge and Ashby's Gap were right before us, swimming in delicate mist. On the right extended a large field, enclosed by a stone fence, in which there was a gate, which seemed to lead into a house beyond the hill.

Across the road lay the dead vidette. His horse was grazing in the high road.

Landon's men swept through the gate, formed column with drawn sabres, and darted onward.

Suddenly a dense smoke rose beyond the hill, — dark, threatening, and tinged with the red glare of flames.

Then we heard on the wind the low and monotonous crackling of a conflagration.

"They are burning the house!" exclaimed Arden.

"No, it is too far to the left," said Landon. "It is the barn and stable; the house will follow, or would."

And, turning in his saddle at full gallop, Landon pointed with his sword to the smoke.

"Do you see?" he said.

A yell answered.

"These people are burning barns and houses, starving women and children! The fewer the prisoners we take the better!"

The men replied with a shout; and, as though driven onward by that shout, the column rushed to the attack.

XXI.

"BEFORE TO-MORROW YOU WILL BE DEAD — OR I WILL."

In a moment, it seemed to me, the little band of Rangers had swept across the extensive field, thundered down a rocky declivity, passed at full gallop through a small stream, and a second gate, and dashed up the hill to the threatened mansion.

It stood upon a knoll, with an emerald slope in front, at the foot of which a weeping willow laved its tassels in the water of a little stream. Around the old portico grew flowers. All had an air of peace, and home, and welcome.

Or would have had, — for the grounds, the portico, the mansion, swarmed with blue coats, whose horses were scattered over the lawn. Half had gone to fire the barn beyond, — a structure containing stalls for fifty horses; half stayed to fire the house. In a dozen hands streaming torches were seen; if we had arrived an instant later, the mansion would have been destroyed. The rush of Landon and his men up the hill was magnificent.

"Charge!" thundered the Rangers.

And at that sound the blue horsemen turned suddenly, and opened fire.

Landon did not pause. In three bounds he was in front of the portico, and his sabre had descended once, twice, thrice, cutting down a man at each stroke.

Then, leaping from his horse, and drawing his pistol with his left hand, — his right still holding his bloody sabre, — he rushed into the mansion.

I followed, and we burst into a large apartment on the right, with a tall mantel-piece, wainscoting, and decorated, at one end, I remember, by the half-length portrait of a gentleman which looked serenely down amid the uproar.

The room was full of Federal soldiers, smashing the glass ware on the sideboard, and tearing open every door in search of plate.

Others were endeavouring to fire the apartment, and in the centre of them I saw Ratcliffe.

Landon rushed upon him, firing as he did so; then, shortening his sword, lunged straight at his heart.

Ratcliffe parried the blow; then bounded backward; and then his men rushed upon Landon and myself, firing and cutting at us. But the tables were quickly turned. The grim faces of the Rangers appeared at the Partisans' back; they threw themselves upon the Federal soldiers, and, in less time than is required to write it, the blue coats had vanished through the rear door of the mansion, and thrown themselves upon their horses.

Landon uttered a sort of growl, and, rushing to his horse, went with drawn sabre on the track of Ratcliffe, who galloped headlong among his flying men.

The Rangers followed, shouting and firing. Then, in front of the burning barn and stables, an obstinate combat ensued, — a wild melée of shots, clashing swords, yells, groans, over which rose the roar of the flames.

Landon had come up with Ratcliffe.

" At last ! " I heard him say, as he closed in with the Federal captain.

And in an instant he was boot to boot with Ratcliffe, had caught him by the throat, and, shortening his sword again, he plunged it I thought through his adversary's breast. I was mistaken. By a quick movement, Ratcliffe evaded the blow, and fired at his opponent, — body to body.

The ball missed its mark, but passed through the throat of the Partisan's horse. The animal uttered a shrill cry, threw up his head, staggered, and fell, dragging down his rider.

But Landon in turn dragged Ratcliffe. Nothing seemed able to make him release his grasp. Clutching the Federal captain by the throat, he dragged him from the saddle, fell upon him, and, half rising, drew back his arm to drive the point of his sabre through his enemy's heart.

Ratcliffe writhed and half rose.

"I surrender!" he cried.

"I'll take no surrender from you, cursed hound!" exclaimed Landon.

But suddenly a whirlwind seemed to sweep over them. Before Landon could stab his adversary, the Federal horse broke in wild flight; passed trampling over the two adversaries; and, rising half stunned to his feet, his face pale, his teeth set, his head uncovered, and with the bleeding marks of hoofs upon his forehead, Landon looked round him.

The Federal cavalry were flying wildly, pursued by the Rangers. At his feet lay Ratcliffe, uttering deep groans.

Landon's laugh replied.

"Good!" he muttered. "I said I would put my hand on you. Before to-morrow you will be dead, or I will!"

XXII.

I WAS close beside Landon when he uttered these words. Never had I seen him look so happy.

"You will fight him?" I said.

"Yes."

"A prisoner?"

"I will release him."

"And his second?"

Landon pointed to a squad of prisoners approaching. Suddenly among them I recognized young Lieutenant Arden, U.S.A., who had exhibited such courage at the house of Miss Annie a few days before.

"There is a lieutenant," said Landon; "he will act as second."

And seeing that Ratcliffe had half risen and was watching him, he said : —

"I refused to give you quarter just now; I now offer it on one condition."

"What condition?" he said, sullenly.

"That you fight me to-night."

"I am bruised — bleeding."

126

"So am I."

And Landon pointed to his bloody forehead.

"Choose!" he added; "either fight or prepare to be shot! I hold no parley with, and have no mercy for, house-burners."

"I will fight you — if paroled," growled Ratcliffe.

Landon looked at him.

"Paroled? — you?"

"Do you doubt my honour, sir?" exclaimed Ratcliffe, starting up.

Landon's expression was indescribable.

"Not at all, sir," he said, coolly; "you are paroled, and will please select your second from the prisoners yonder. Colonel Surry, will you be good enough to act for me?"

I bowed and looked toward Ratcliffe.

He recognized me and scowled bitterly.

"Ah! I see you remember me, my dear Captain Ratcliffe," I said, laughing. "I am still riding your horse, — an excellent one. But your second?"

"Lieutenant Arden," he said, sullenly, pointing to the young officer.

I bowed again, and went and introduced myself to Lieutenant Arden, U.S.A., who received me with great politeness. It is impossible to imagine anything more tranquil than his demeanour. He told with a smile that his horse had been shot under him, his sabre cut from his side, his pistol knocked from his hand, and "they had ended by riding over him, and demanding his surrender."

"Whereupon you surrendered, lieutenant?" I said, laughing.

"Of course," he replied, with a smile.

"Well, you did not do so the other night, on your visit to a young lady of our acquaintance."

And I pointed toward the Opequon.

"Were you there?" he exclaimed.

"Yes, but not among your opponents."

"A queer affair. They ought to have killed me. My visit was unlucky."

"Your visit?"

"To the young lady. Is she a friend of yours, colonel?"

He smiled and glanced at me curiously.

"Don't fight me!" he said. "I went to carry her a pass through the lines, which I heard she wished. I have seen her but once before, and I did not know — "

He paused and sighed.

"That your brother loved her?"

He looked at me.

"You know all, I see. Well, colonel, so be it. At least you now understand why it would have been stupid to have been killed that night. Unjust, too. I was doing a good action."

And seeing *our* Arden approach, the prisoner went to him and said, laughing : —

" How are you, Harry ? "

The young man leaped from his horse and threw his arms round his brother's neck.

Blue and gray were clasped tight in each other's arms !

When they drew back I think there were tears in the eyes of both.   Then, bowing toward me : —

" At your orders, colonel," said Lieutenant Arden, U.S.A.

9

XXIII.

BIZARRE.

THE terms of the combat between Landon and Ratcliffe were speedily arranged by myself and Lieutenant Arden, whom I found to be a perfect gentleman.

Pistols were chosen; the meeting was to take place at a spot on the banks of the Shenandoah, called "Lover's Leap," near which Landon designed to bivouac that night, and the hour determined upon was daylight next morning.

Having perfected these arrangements with Lieutenant Arden, U.S.A., I made that gentleman a bow, and, turning him over to his brother, who was plainly dying to talk to him, returned and reported to Landon.

"A thousand thanks, colonel," he said, quietly; and Ratcliffe, having been supplied with a captured horse, Landon, who had mounted another, began to move with his troop toward the Blue Ridge.

The result of the combat had been a few prisoners and many dead bodies in blue. Landon's loss was half a dozen wounded. Behind us smouldered the black ruin.

The little body of horsemen slowly took their way toward the Shenandoah. Winding along through a secluded glen, studded with mossy rocks, they passed through a gate in the stone fence, turned to the left, and, following a shaded road, made their way through the country between Millwood and White Post.

Oh, the lovely region as we rode on, that September! Oh, the trees touched with gold, and the mountains bathed in azure! It was a land all romance, you would have said, gentle reader, where the graces danced, and the loves disported. Nothing stirred the air but the winds in the forest, the music of cascades, and the murmur of the Shenandoah beneath its sycamores.

Nothing else? Hear that muttering from the direction of Winchester! It is Early's war-dogs growling, and showing Sheridan their teeth. Loves and graces? Look at these figures, bearded and grim, — the figures in gray and blue. Murmuring waterfalls? You hear the rattle of the sabre!

But the land was beautiful if the red hoof had stamped upon it. It is beautiful to-day, and will be beautiful forever; for the blue mountains yonder are laughing at factions, parties, and intrigues in 1868, as they echoed, with hoarse laughter, in their fir-

clad gorges, the roar of the cannon, in that strange
year 1864.

As the sun was sinking toward the forest we saw
the "Blue Ball," as a peak of the mountain is
called, right before us, and the voice of the river
ascended in a low murmur from its bed hundreds of
feet beneath us.

On a hill rose an old and very stately-looking
mansion. Landon pointed to it and said : —

"This is my house, 'Bizarre,' colonel. I am
glad to have you visit it."

A ride of fifteen minutes brought us in front of
the old mansion,—a building of large size, with something "aristocratic" about it. Pardon that obso-
lete, old-fashioned phrase, reader.

"Bizarre" seemed to have been the residence of
many generations of gentlemen. Half in ruins, as
it was, there was something proud and imposing in
its worn *façade*. You could see that men and
women had held high revelry here in the old days
when Virginia was Virginia.

At a sign from Landon the men broke ranks and
scattered themselves through the extensive grounds,
with only videttes out. Landon calculated rightly
that few Federals would venture to penetrate these
great woods.

Captain Ratcliffe and Lieutenant Ralph Arden
were ushered into the mansion, where an old negro,

who seemed to be the genius of the place, hastened, by Landon's order, to provide supper for them. They were not placed under guard, having both given their paroles not to attempt to escape; and, making *his guests* a low bow, Landon went out of the apartment.

I was beside him, and we found ourselves in the great hall of the mansion. It was inexpressibly bare and desolate. Old portraits mouldered on the walls. From some huge deer-antlers hung cobwebs. The spider was lord here, and reigned in joint sovereignty with the mouse and the moth.

"A deserted old affair this," said the Partisan, coolly. "Those tall-backed chairs, colonel, and these dingy old pictures, are all that remain to me, except the bare walls."

"You have been away for years, I suppose?"

"Yes, and feel almost like a stranger."

He gazed around him with an abstracted look. An expression of sadness would have visited the countenance of most men. Landon seemed to have no room in his heart for so gentle an emotion. Was this man made of marble? I tried to test him.

"You are the last of your line, captain?" I said.

"Yes; the last."

"It is sorrowful."

"Many things are sorrowful in this world, colonel."

"You have no brothers or sisters?"

"None."

"And your parents, — your family?"

"All gone. My mother was the last, and she died some years since."

The marble was touched. A faint tinge came to Landon's cheeks.

"I loved my mother," he said, in a low voice; "and they murdered her!"

A quick flash of the eye followed. Turning his head, in a manner inexpressibly stern and haughty, he glanced toward the apartment occupied by Ratcliffe.

"That man was her murderer," he said. "Do you wonder now that I hate him?"

His brows were knit together; a grim smile came to his lips.

"Luckily, I have one consolation," he said, in his cool voice. "Like Randolph of Roanoke, I am the last of my house; I am alone in the world, without father or mother, brother or sister; I am a mere waif, an estray, — a stranger here in the halls of my forefathers; but good fortune has not wholly deserted me. I have the man I hate most in this world within a few yards of me, — in twelve hours, or less, will stand facing him, when I hope to settle, once for all, our little account."

Landon's vibrating and metallic voice ceased, and his glance wandered to a portrait on the wall. It represented a lady of great beauty and distinction, with blue eyes, and brown hair piled up upon the forehead; one white jewelled hand was raised to the head-dress. In the whole portrait there was something exquisitely high-bred and delicate.

As he continued to gaze at this picture, the colour upon Landon's cheeks gradually deepened; his lips were compressed as though to arrest a sob; in his fiery eye glittered something like a tear.

"I thought I was strong," he muttered; "but that face makes me a child again!"

"Your mother?"

He turned quickly.

"Yes, colonel, my poor mother! She left me last, and that finished me."

His head sank. A grim contraction of the brows betrayed the hidden anguish. All at once he turned his head and looked at me.

"All this must seem strange to you," he said, "and I fear you think me something of a charlatan."

"Captain!"

"Only charlatans or outcasts change their names; conceal themselves; have mysteries."

"Why speak thus bitterly?" I said. "Do you imagine I ever thought thus of you? Your face is enough, Captain Landon; it is a loyal face."

He made me the bow of a nobleman.

"Thanks! I value your good opinion," he said. "But I have appeared to you under peculiar circumstances, colonel. You saw me at Manassas under a different name; you come hither and hear Miss Adair address me, as she did yonder, in a manner not very complimentary. Well, all this must appear rather 'mysterious' to you, as the novel-writers say, and I have little fondness for mystery."

"Well, I acknowledge that *I* have," I said, smiling.

Landon was silent; he evidently hesitated. His dark eyes interrogated my face.

"I am heavy-hearted to-night," he said, suddenly, in his deep voice. "We have fought together. You are a comrade, — a gentleman. Would you like to hear a rather curious story, friend, to while away an hour this evening?"

I extended my hand and grasped Landon's.

"*Your* story? That is a mark of friendship you give me."

He inclined his head.

"You are right, colonel; but it will be a relief to *me*. To-night, thought seems to crush me. You will listen?"

"Speak, captain! You do me an honour and a pleasure."

"Then follow me, colonel. There is a spot near this house which I have not visited for years, — the scene of the duel to-morrow, — and it is connected with the events which I am going briefly to relate. Let us go thither; it is but a step."

"You mean the 'Lover's Leap'?"

"Yes."

And, leading the way, Landon left the mansion. I followed him in silence.

XXIV.

LOVER'S LEAP.

WE passed through the extensive grounds, descended a grassy slope, and my companion led the way into a dense forest of pines, which he threaded by a path which seemed well known to him.

Passing beneath the lofty dome of foliage, from the summit of which the sinking sun was slowly lifting up the golden crown, we continued to follow the path; the wood opened; nearly opposite was the shaggy "Blue Ball;" fifty yards further we suddenly emerged upon a precipice, at the far base of which rolled the waves of the Shenandoah, and from whose summit the eye swept a lovely landscape of lofty mountain and winding river, bathed in the golden light of sunset.

"Lover's Leap" was a rude mass of rock, which we approached by a narrow path half covered with a carpet of pine tassels. On the very brink of the precipice grew a solitary pine, by clasping which you could lean far over the dizzy verge and see the Shenandoah hundreds of feet beneath you. All around rose the fir-clad slopes; beyond the river

138

smiling fields stretched away to the base of the Blue Ridge, whose forests were of every colour of the rainbow.

Landon took his seat upon a mass of rock near the solitary pine, and passed his hand over his forehead.

The gesture was gloomy; but the Partisan's lip wore the cool, impassive expression which was habitual with him.

"Do you know what I think sometimes, colonel?" he said.

"What?"

"That life is a farce, — existence a bore at best."

"Then I know you are not happy."

"You are wrong there."

"I am truly glad to hear it."

"Have I not something to put me in high good humour?"

"Ah! you mean —"

"Exactly! It is charming to be understood, colonel. Yes, I have the little affair with Ratcliffe; and, as I have been longing for it lately, I ought to feel the tranquil satisfaction of a man who has attained, or is about to attain, the object of his wishes."

Landon uttered a low laugh. It was not a pleasant sound.

"Why not?" he continued. "Am I not fortunate? Men are charmed when they have the woman they love beside them, — when they can say, 'I love you,' and hear her reply, 'I will marry you.' Why should I not be gratified, then, when I have my dear enemy beside me?—can say to him, 'I hate you,' and hear him reply, 'I will fight you?' Tastes vary in this world, colonel. Some men, no doubt, would prefer the interview with their lady-love; I prefer that with my enemy. Others thrill at, 'I will marry you!' I am charmed with, 'I will fight you!'"

I looked curiously at this man.

"I can understand, — or think I will, — when you tell me your story."

"Well, you shall have it, friend. I am not a confiding personage generally, but something moves me to-night."

And, leaning back against the great rock, Landon thus continued : —

"I was born at 'Bizarre,' — the old house which you have visited to-night, — and grew to the age of eighteen without ever leaving home. My father died in my childhood, leaving one other son and two daughters, all younger than myself.

"Well, at eighteen I spent a year at the Virginia Military Institute, preparing for West Point, whither my father had expressed a wish that I should go. He fancied that I had betrayed an early aptitude for the army, and, on his death-bed, had shaped out my future. My mother, who doted on her children, was bitterly opposed to this step; but I urged my father's wishes; set out joyfully for Lexington; and duly became a cadet.

"Here commenced my acquaintance with the person with whom I am going to fight to-morrow morning,— Ratcliffe. He was from East Tennessee, about the same age as myself, and we soon became intimate, — for what reason I have never been able to understand. These things happen. The court which Ratcliffe paid to me, perhaps, explained the fact. He had taken up, I discovered afterwards, the impression that I was extremely rich, — the heir of an 'old family' of high position, — and, as he was a person of humble birth, and aspiring, he looked to me, it seems, to aid his career.

"Well, his attentions won me. For the rest, I was open and confiding then. We became intimate; he informed me that he had secured an appointment and was going to West Point; and, as I had also been appointed, we arranged to go northward together.

"When I was about to return home, Ratcliffe said, carelessly, that he was half resolved to go and spend the interval with me, instead of returning to Tennessee. I responded by a cordial invitation; he accepted at once; and in a few days we were at 'Bizarre,' — two youths, full of life and health, 'home for the holidays.'

" This brief recital will show you, colonel, how
Ratcliffe — a stranger to this region and to our people here — became mixed up with my life. I can
look back now and see what I could not then; that
he had used a hundred acts to become intimate with
me, and secure this invitation. Cunning, ambitious,
obscure, he aimed to rise from his low sphere by
social 'connections,' and his first step had succeeded;
he had become an inmate of ' Bizarre,' the associate
of my mother and my sisters.

" They did not like him. My mother was a person of great simplicity and sweetness, but of very
high breeding; and I soon saw that something in
Ratcliffe displeased her. As to the girls, nothing
could induce them to smile upon him. I resented
this, as you may imagine; took my friend everywhere; made him acquainted with the most agreeable
young ladies of the region, and, among others, with
Miss Adair, whom you met at the Old Chapel that
night.

" From her childhood, Miss Adair had been — to
use the English phrase — my ' sweetheart.' My
father and Judge Adair had been intimate friends;
our mothers old schoolmates, and very much devoted
to each other. Thus to fall in love with Miss Ellen
Adair seemed the simplest and easiest thing in the
world to the boy, St. Leger Landon, who burned to
cement the affection of father for father, mother for

mother, by marrying the young lady, and thus perfecting the union of the two families.

"When I went to Lexington I was already engaged to the young lady; on my return, I saw, at our first meeting, that her feelings had undergone no change; and before I left 'Chapeldale,' her father's residence, — you have been there, — our engagement was renewed, and rendered more binding than before. In other words, Miss Adair had solemnly plighted me her troth, — promised that she would marry me, — and I returned to 'Bizarre' so perfectly happy that I thought fate itself was powerless to overcloud a sky as radiant as my future."

A bitter smile came to Landon's lips.

"Such is youth," he went on. "It believes everything, and takes no account of that terrible 'element of failure,' which mingles with every human undertaking. If any one had told me then that this beautiful girl, with the truthful eyes and the smiling lips, would break my heart (excuse that cant, colonel, it is expressive); that she would shipwreck me for a fancy, a chimera, without listening to my defence, I would have laughed, and considered the joke excellent!"

Landon's countenance, as he uttered these words, was inexpressibly cynical and bitter. For a man to smile as the young Partisan smiled, it was necessary to have passed through much and great suffering.

That suffering he had evidently endured; it was caused by a woman, and I listened with profound interest and attention to the deep voice which told me everything.

Landon paused for an instant; a grim contraction of the brows followed; a shadow seemed to pass across his forehead; but he continued his narrative in a voice which indicated no emotion of any description whatever.

XXV.

POISON.

"I took Ratcliffe, as I have informed you, to visit the family at 'Chapeldale,' and, having thus been introduced, he went thither frequently afterwards, not seldom by himself. I did not dream of his becoming my rival. My rival? The thing was impossible! Had I not informed him of my engagement; grown extravagant, as young men will, over my love, my adoration, my infatuation for Miss Adair? How was it possible for *a gentleman* to think of wooing his friend's *affiancée?* Well, I swear to you, the thought never entered my head, until one morning Miss Adair quietly said : —

"'You have a singular friend.'

"'Singular?' I said.

"'Yes,' was her reply. 'He addressed me yesterday; you ought to know it.'

"She looked frightened, as she glanced at my face.

"'Good heavens! how pale you are!' she said; 'you are angry?'

" ' No,' I replied, and ten minutes afterwards I left her.

" I went back at a gallop to ' Bizarre,' hastened to Ratcliffe's room, entered, and charged him with his perfidy. His reply was a good-humoured laugh, and the words : —

" ' Why, old fellow, can't you allow an inveterate *flirt* like myself to have some fun without wanting to cut my throat for it? Do you think I for a moment imagined I could cut you out with Miss Ellen? that I was in earnest? You are too sensitive, old fellow, too distrustful.' And for ten minutes he poured out his smiling blandishments and denials; laughing, and finally putting me in a good humour again.

" ' Well, Ratcliffe,' I said, ' I will say no more about this, but on one condition, — a condition which I exact.'

" ' What is that? ' he said, smiling.

" ' That you will never utter another word of that description to Miss Adair as long as you live.'

" ' And if I decline,' he said, laughing.

" Those words fired me.

" ' Try it,' I said, 'and by Heaven, I will have your blood ! '

" He turned white as I spoke, and a flash of anger darted from his eye. A moment afterwards he forced a laugh, and said : —

" ' All right, old fellow; but you don't mean to deny me the privilege of calling on Miss Ellen ? '

" ' Certainly not,' I replied, already growing ashamed of uttering such harsh words to a guest; ' but I have your promise, you understand ? '

" ' All right,' he repeated, laughing as before; and the interview terminated.

"Going to my room," continued Landon, " I sat down and reflected. Had I not been harsh and uncharitable toward Ratcliffe? The young lady doubtless exaggerated his attentions, misunderstood mere ' gallantry,' and did not know that, by many of her sex, such avowals as Ratcliffe had made were regarded simply as an amusing pastime, meaning little. Thus I gradually regained my equanimity, and when I again saw Miss Adair, informed her, with a smile, that I doubted extremely whether Ratcliffe was as much in love with her as she imagined. It was a brilliant jest, you see; but I do not think the young lady relished it very much. She replied that her imagination had had nothing to do with the matter. And as this incident occurred just as Ratcliffe and myself were about to set off for West Point, I had the misery of parting with the young lady in a frame of mind far less agreeable than I desired. Have you ever been what is called ' in love,' friend? If so, I need not tell you that to leave the woman you love with no smile upon her lips, no light in her eyes, is not agreeable. It was thus I left her, to go to West Point. Something like a cloud seemed to have swept across the sky overshadowing the landscape. In the sequel, as you will perceive, events were to occur which blackened the whole horizon of my life.

" I now approach the main point of my narrative. Many things remain a mystery still to me, but subsequent information revealed to me an amount of *diablerie* on the part of my dear friend Ratcliffe, which will be sufficient to give interest to my story. Many things I know ; what I do not know, I suspect. You shall judge if I have cause to love this man.

" To relate all in its order. I went to West Point, leaving my mother, my sisters, and my younger brother in perfect health. Six months afterwards the whole family were attacked with pneumonia; my brother and both my sisters died, and my mother was brought to the brink of the grave. I hastened back at the first intelligence of their illness, only in time to follow the funeral cortege of the last of my sisters to the Old Chapel; then for a month I watched, breathless, the progress of my mother's malady.

" Well, she rallied at length. I had the inexpressible happiness of seeing the colour return to her cheeks. Her constitution was evidently broken, but at least she was spared to me ! From that moment she became a thousand times dearer to me; and the love which she gave me in return even exceeded my own for her.

"Alas!" said Landon, with flushed cheeks, and sighing wearily, "men do not know the happiness of having a mother until she is dead! Then they bitterly repent all their waywardness, their neglect, their absence without reason. They would give all they possess to feel the pressure of the thin hand on their heated brows again, to hear the dear mother's voice, and see the old, fond, caressing smile!"

The man's heart throbbed, and his lips trembled as he spoke. This memory of his mother had flushed his cheeks as he gazed at her portrait, and agitated him again as he now spoke of her. It seemed the sole tie which still bound him to his species, and kept the heart of this iceberg from freezing.

"I loved my mother," he groaned, with something like a fiery tear in the haughty eyes. "No man ever loved mother more, and that wretch yonder was the cause of her death!"

His face grew hard again as he referred to Ratcliffe. In his eye was the old, grim, pitiless look; the glance of the man whose purpose is not to be shaken.

"Listen, friend," he went on coolly, "and I will tell you how Ratcliffe thus darkened my whole life. The fact was long a mystery to me; it is only re-

cently that I have discovered the deep debt I owe
him, and I hope to repay him to the last farthing.
Some men's memories are short, and lose everything ; mine is long, and loses nothing.

"To narrate.   I returned to West Point after the
death of my brother and sisters, and the illness of
my mother, almost broken down in spirits.   One
thing alone consoled me;— the fond and faithful affection of the young girl to whom I had given my
whole heart.   Her love had never failed me; seemed
to deepen rather, as she saw how much I suffered ;
and the recollection of the tenderness which she exhibited for me at that time has alone preserved me
from the darkest cynicism, the intensest scorn and
hatred for her whole sex.   When I parted with her,
there was no cloud upon the pure and truthful brow;
in her heart there was nothing but love for me.   It
was arranged that we were to be married as soon as
I attained my majority ; and with this to console me
and light up my poor weary life, I returned to finish
my course at West Point.

"I remained there until the autumn of 1860.
Then the storm began to mutter, and it was plain
that the Republicans would attempt to coerce the
South if she dared to secede from the Union. Would
the Southern States do so ?   South Carolina — the
brave, the chivalrous South Carolina — first drew
the sword and threw away the scabbard; Virginia

was plainly going to follow. As to her action I never doubted; as to my own course, I did not hesitate. I never yet knew the time when the flag of Virginia was not my flag before all others; when I did not consider myself bound to obey the order of the Governor of Virginia before that of the President of the United States; when I did not say to myself, 'I am a citizen first and foremost of the sovereign nation of Virginia, and only afterwards *a sort of* citizen of the political federation called the United States.'

"But I weary you. To return: I came back to Virginia in the autumn of 1860, to offer her my sword; and I never saw Ratcliffe again until the other day. He declared his intention of remaining at the North, and 'taking no part in the rebellion,' — and this alone would have broken our connection. We had already grown cold, however, and even quarrelled on other grounds, — the result simply of the man's utter depravity and want of principle. I have never set myself up as an example to anybody, colonel, and have never had the pretension to make broad my phylacteries, and thank God I am not as yonder sinner. On the contrary, I lived freely, — drank, played cards, and was far from a model. But Ratcliffe was a thousand times worse, and absolutely revolted me. Drunkenness, insane gambling, debauchery of every description, were habitual with him. To this he added a laxity in money matters, and a facility in breaking his word, which gradually alienated me from him, and ended by terminating our intimacy.

" Then, as I have since discovered, he began to hate me, and had a double reason to ruin me if he could. Do you ask the meaning of the word ' double ' ? My reply is that he was crazily in love with Miss Adair, — a fact which I have discovered, like the rest, only recently.

" This, then, was the ' situation,' as we say in the army. I was engaged to Miss Adair. Ratcliffe loved her, and hated me. Obviously, to ruin me would be to gratify at once his love and his vengeance. And he nearly accomplished his object.

" I come now to the most curious portion of my story, — Ratcliffe's mode of proceeding in undermining my character and good name in an entire community. His course was one full of strange cunning. By letters, both anonymous and over his signature, he disseminated the most frightful calumnies in reference to me. I have seen some of these letters, and it is impossible to convey to you any idea of the diabolical ingenuity of the writer. I was represented as a monster. My small vices were magnified into gigantic crimes ; my chance games at cards into wild gambling ; my occasional wine-drinking into brutal drunkenness. I was charged with such other vices as degrade and brutalize young men, — with utter falsehood, for I was innocent; and the whole portrait thus drawn was so repulsive and hateful, that those who did not know me must have shrunk in horror and disgust from the moral monster thus presented to their view.

"When I returned to the Valley in 1860, Ratcliffe had accomplished his object, or a portion of it. My best friends turned away from or looked coldly at me. Does that seem fanciful, colonel? Bah! nothing that is mean is fanciful in human nature! Do you think that the world is not pleased when you stumble? *They* are standing erect and are better than you! Do you think that your 'friends' believe with difficulty discreditable reports about you? Undeceive yourself; they hasten to believe them, and I assure you they lose no time in disseminating them, — to communicate 'bad news' is so delightful! 'No news is good news,' the proverb says, — that is, people never take the trouble to communicate what will make you happy; but let them only have some bad news that will make you miserable, — you shall know that, if they have to arouse you at midnight!

' "Well, many persons had shocking news to tell of the reprobate St. Leger Landon, the drunkard, the debauchee, the unprincipled blackguard! It was all communicated under the breath, in whispers, — in the 'giggle-gabble' tone, — and the whole air was poisoned. At tea-drinkings, church, court, everywhere, people shook their heads, groaned, lamented the shocking conduct of the last of the Landons — and pitied my poor mother.

"My mother! there was where the arrow struck. Of Miss Adair I will speak presently; but first of my mother. The kind friends whom I have mentioned did not fail to put her in possession of the reports in relation to me; they would not have missed the luxury of seeing her writhe, and of witnessing her agony. They came to ' Bizarre;' had no pity for her pale face and trembling nerves; struck her cruelly, pitilessly, as women can only strike women, and ended by prostrating her upon a bed of illness. The implacable fury of the old gossips had pierced the tender heart to its core, and she was overwhelmed. Since I, her only child, her stay and comfort, had become thus depraved, there was no longer anything in life worth living for; existence was a burden.

" Can you realize from these cold, colourless words, the spectacle which greeted me upon my return? It was that of my mother, stretched upon the couch from which she was never more to rise, writhing under the poisonous stings of those female tongues,— believing that her only boy, her all, was worse than dead to her! That was what greeted me as I came back to ' Bizarre' with open arms to kiss my dear mother!

"Three months afterwards she was dead. The shock to her system from the loss of her children, and all this painful emotion in addition, had brought on a return of her malady. This second attack she had not been able to withstand. I followed her to the Old Chapel graveyard, as I had followed my brother and my sisters."

XXVI.

NAMELESS.

WITH compressed lips Landon resumed his narrative.

"I had already parted forever with Miss Adair. That abrupt announcement probably surprises you, and I will briefly relate the particulars of this somewhat curious occurrence. Up to the latter months of my stay at West Point, no change had taken place in my relations with the young lady. Our correspondence had continued uninterrupted. Her letters were all that I could wish, and when the intelligence of my brother's and sisters' illness brought me back to 'Bizarre,' I had found in her love, as I have said, my greatest comfort. So much for my affair up to the last few months of my absence.

"Then everything changed. In her letters I began to discern that indefinable something which cannot be described, but which indicates a change of feeling, as the atmosphere indicates an approaching storm. I could not define this; it eluded my vigilance when I attempted to touch it; but it was there! The love was all gone out of the heart behind the hand that wrote! The next letter I received was positively chilling. I wrote, demanding an explanation. None came. I wrote again. The response was a sheet of paper enveloping the young lady's engagement ring. Upon the sheet was written : —

"'Our correspondence and acquaintance end here and now. It will be useless to attempt a renewal of either.'

"I remember the words perfectly. There are certain things written or uttered in this world which burn their impress upon the heart and memory, and are ineffaceable. Spoken, you hear them long years afterward. Written, you see, when a quarter of a century has passed, the very page which contained them, and across which they seemed dashed in flame!

"'*Our correspondence and acquaintance end here and now!*'

"Did I hold a pen in my hand, with a sheet of paper before me, I could trace with perfect accuracy the shape of every letter in that sentence as she traced them! I recall the appearance of the words, as a man recalls the page that he read when labouring under some frightful grief.

"What made her write thus to me? Why did this honest and true heart strike *my* heart so piti-

lessly, and overthrow in an instant the whole fabric
which I had been building in the future? Why
did Ellen Adair thus insult, outrage, ruin the man
who loved her more than he loved his own life?
That is still a mystery to me. Was it the result of
Ratcliffe's cowardly calumnies? It is hard to believe so, and yet what could have come between us
but that? What other arts did he use? What
means did he employ? This is still the mystery of
mysteries to me, and I can only attribute the young
lady's action to the discreditable reports in regard to
me, since she denied me all opportunity of defend-
ing myself.

"This surprises you; and it is more than sur-
prising, — it is incredible. Truth is generally incredible. But I will narrate the plain facts, without
comment : —

"Well, I raged when I read that letter, and for
days was the victim of the cruellest despair. What
should I do? Write again? My pride revolted
from thus lowering myself and coming back, like a
whipped hound, to receive another cut of the lash!
Friend, my theory in this world is, that an honourable
gentleman gives much when he gives his whole heart;
that a young lady owes him something in return,—
some consideration; that she does wrong in acting
as though all the giving were upon her side alone,
and his love a trifling affair in comparison with her

caprice ! I loved this young lady ; but that did not give her the right to outrage me thus wantonly, —to strike me cruelly, mercilessly, with insult, to the very heart. Well, I swore that I would not write a line in reply, — and I did not.

"But I writhed terribly. I was not a philosopher, only a young man very much in love, and the steel pierced me to the heart. I determined to wait until I saw Miss Adair in person, and I saw her when I came to Virginia in the autumn of 1860. Shall I describe my reception, or rather how I was not even received ? No sooner had I arrived at ' Bizarre ' and embraced my mother, than I ordered my horse, set out at full speed, passed through Millwood without drawing rein, and soon found myself at Chapeldale.

"' Judge Adair was not at home,' a servant informed me, as I threw myself from my horse, and hastened up the steps of the mansion. Judge Adair ? I did not wish to see Judge Adair, I responded ; where was Miss Adair ? The servant looked confused. He would go and inquire, he said. He went, remained away a few minutes, and returning, said, ' Miss Ellen begged to be excused, —she had a headache.' I remember staring vacantly in the face of the old gray-haired servant, who knew and loved me ; his agitation and confusion were greater than my own even. Then I flushed to the temples, wheeled abruptly, and went away furious, resolved that I would never return.

"I returned on the next day. Cold and stern, expecting my fate, and looking it in the face, I again knocked at the door. The same old gray-haired servant appeared, and I again asked for the young lady. This time he had not to leave me in order to go and receive Miss Adair's response to my summons. With a countenance which indicated the deepest respect and sympathy, the old servant delivered the message with which he had been intrusted. My visit had thus been foreseen, and Miss Adair evidently intended that it should be the last. This time there was no allusion made to a headache. Miss Adair's response in advance, to my morning call, was simply to the effect that it was not her intention to come downstairs and see Mr. St. Leger Landon.

"Well, that ended everything, you see. I listened to the words quietly, left the mansion, and, mounting my horse, returned to 'Bizarre,' swearing in my heart that I would never again darken the doors of a house in which I had been wantonly outraged; and this time I have kept my oath. From that time to the other day, or night rather, at the Chapel, I have never even seen the young lady, nor do I ever intend again to see her if I can avoid it.

"Enough of that; let me finish my sorrowful

history, colonel. This final rupture with Miss Adair took place as soon as I reached Virginia; but a few weeks afterwards events occurred at 'Bizarre' which made me lose sight of all else. My mother's illness, pneumonia, combined with a nervous disorder, produced by these calumnies which I have mentioned, grew rapidly more threatening. A month afterwards she was evidently sinking; and one night, when she placed her feeble arms around me, I felt her head fall upon my bosom, — she was dead!"

Landon uttered a hoarse sob as he spoke, and turned away. Something in my own throat seemed choking me. To witness the emotion of this man of marble was a terrible spectacle.

"You see they had killed her!" he muttered in a low, deep voice; "they had told her I was a wretch, and broken her heart. True, a word from me had been sufficient to brand that lie, and undo the whole devilish plot against me. The mother's heart was soft, if the heart of my betrothed was hard; but the work was done, and my poor, fond mother had no more strength even to be happy! She died in my arms, with her head upon my bosom, and sleeps yonder in the Old Chapel, where I hope some day to lie beside her.

"Well, such were the events of the fall and winter of 1860, colonel. I was alone at 'Bizarre,' a mere wreck, no longer like myself. A double chord

11

had snapped in my breast, and I was desperate.
First had come the terrible result of my affair with
Miss Adair: the woman I loved had thrown me away
like a worthless glove, split and useless; and, dead
as she was to me, attempt as I might to forget her,
every object reminded me of her; everything re-
called her. At 'Bizarre,' where she had been often,
for she was a great favourite with my mother, there
was scarce a piece of furniture, a book, a wicker
chair on the lawn, which I did not associate with
her. Over every walk we had strolled together,
over every country road we had ridden, and here, at
Lover's Leap, we had twenty times conversed.
Here, sitting on this very rock, she looked at me as
women only look at the men they love; here her
delicious voice had rung clearly in the sunset, and
we had passed long hours, with the pines whispering
above, the river murmuring beneath, watching the
clouds which floated over us, all gold in the light of
sunset. I loved that woman! God help me, but I
believe I love her still!"

Landon paused, his cheeks glowing, his eyes
flashing.

"Good!" he said in a moment, with his sardonic
smile. "I am growing poetical, colonel. I am talking about eyes and sighs; let us leave all that flum-
mery, and come back to events. My narrative will
be ended very soon now.

" The last blow, as I said, was my mother's death, and I dare not attempt to describe the void left by *that.* I can tell you how I missed everywhere the presence of the woman I loved; but I cannot speak of my feelings when I looked round the old deserted house of ' Bizarre,' and heard a voice say, ' Your mother is gone ! ' You can replace your betrothed, even your wife,— that happens, though I think it would not to me,— but there is something which you cannot replace, — the smile of the face which bent over you when you were a helpless babe in arms. God gives that once, and only once. And he had taken it from me forever.

" Well, in the spring of 1861, things had come to a bad pass with me. My mother was dead; the woman I loved had thrown me away; I was alone, — seemed even to have no friends. On all sides I saw cold looks, heard cold voices, and touched cold hands. I cared little; grief had stunned me; but the strange fact was that I could not discover the origin of this coldness, or solve the mystery. Everybody avoided me; I was an outlaw, apparently, and at last the pride and disdain of my character rose up and spurred me to a wild rage. I tried to find some one to insult and fight; but, alas ! I had not even that consolation. I could find no enemy, only people who bowed coldly; and I went back to ' Bizarre,' torn by wrath, misery, and despair. That dishonour should be imputed to a descendant of the Landons! That my father's son should be supposed even to have soiled his noble name! The thought was bitter, almost intolerable.

"I writhed under it; then the war broke out. I joined the army; and you now know, colonel, why I took my mother's name of St. Leger, under which you first met me. To that name, at least, I was entitled.

"The rest of my story need not detain you. I had just received my commission of captain of cavalry, a year ago, when we rode together through the barricade near Manassas. You will ask what had become of Ratcliffe. The response is easy. He had always been northern in his sentiments; remained at West Point and graduated; joined the enemy, and was sent to serve in Missouri, where I heard he was killed in 1862.

"To end my narrative. Tired of the regular service, I resigned my commission last spring; raised a company of Partisans, and came to operate against Sheridan in the Valley here. With my former friends I have had nothing to do; from the first I held myself aloof from them; but one of them stopped me one day, and kindly volunteered at the eleventh hour to state a few facts for my information. Then I knew, for the first time, the extent of my obligations to Ratcliffe. My informant not

only laid bare the plot against me, but exhibited two
or three letters in Ratcliffe's handwriting, which, if
believed, were sufficient to ruin me a hundred times
in the estimation of virtuous people. That was a
month or two ago. You were present at the skirmish yonder when I found that Ratcliffe was not
dead; crossed sabres with him; and came near settling our account with him then and there. What
has followed you know. At last my foe is in my
power: he shall fight me fairly, man to man, in honourable combat; but before that combat takes place,
I shall have a private interview with him, — an interview in which many things will be discussed, I
promise you.

"Enough, colonel," said Landon; "let us return;
I am anxious to look after my dear guest. I took
his parole with repugnance, and under compulsion;
I distrust him. Were he to break it, I would miss
one of the few enjoyments that I promise myself in
life, — that of standing face to face with him, and
sending a bullet or a sword's point through the
cowardly heart that has worked my misery!"

Suddenly rapid hoof-strokes resounded from the
pines in the direction of the mansion; and one of the
Rangers appeared, approaching at full speed.

"What is it?" said Landon, quickly.

"The Yankee captain has escaped!" exclaimed
the man.

" Escaped ! "

And Landon rose erect with one bound, his eyes flaming.

" Yes, captain. You know he was paroled. Well, he walked out coolly to the woods, mounted a horse, and was half a mile off before we knew it. A dozen of us chased him, but he got off."

Landon's teeth were set together; his brows contracted.

" And the lieutenant ? " he said; " he was also paroled."

" He is all right, captain. He says the Yankee captain is a liar and a coward."

Landon's lip curled bitterly.

" I could have told him that," he muttered.

And, turning to me : —

" Come, colonel," he said, " let us go back. The indulgence of this fit of egotism has cost me dear ! "

XXVII.

In five minutes we were again at "Bizarre."

On the porch of the mansion stood Lieutenant Ralph Arden, his brow gloomy, his arms folded, and I have never seen an expression of deeper shame and mortification upon human countenance.

"Place me under guard, Captain Landon!" he said, abruptly, as we approached. "That man has dishonoured himself — his uniform — me — every officer in the Federal army! You paroled him to meet you in honourable combat; he has sneaked off like a coward; and I was his second! He has broken his parole like a vulgar blackguard! *I*, too, am paroled; I may break mine! I surrender that parole — now — instantly!"

Landon looked keenly at the young officer.

"You are Harry Arden's brother?" he said.

"I am."

"That is enough. Mount your horse and report to General Early at Winchester."

An obstinate shake of the head was the young officer's reply.

167

"You refuse?"

"I do."

"So be it. Lieutenant Arden, you will be responsible for your brother to-night. To-morrow I will send him under guard to Winchester."

And Landon entered the mansion, silent and gloomy. I remained behind with the young men.

"O Harry!" I heard the young Federal officer say, — his brows contracted, his eyes wet with tears of shame, — "that ever I should come to this, and be thus degraded!"

And like one "refusing to be comforted" the unfortunate victim of the astute Ratcliffe turned away in silence.

"Well, guard me, Harry!" he added, with a bitter smile; "who knows but I may trick you and escape before morning?"

And, leaning on the shoulder of his brother, he entered the house.

An hour afterward I had thrown myself on a couch, wrapped my cape around me, and was asleep. The last sounds which I heard were the voices of the two brothers, as they murmured a hundred recollections of youth and home. There was an unspeakably tender music in the accents of the two youths, as there was something strangely pathetic in their fate. To-morrow they might meet each other, sabre to sabre, and shed each other's blood; to-night they were whispering, like children, in each other's arms !

On the next morning Harry Arden formally reported with his prisoner to Landon, and the prisoner still insisting upon surrendering his parole, he was despatched under guard of two men to Early's headquarters.

The three left "Bizarre" about noon. At six in the evening a melancholy and "shame-faced" pair of Night-Hawks reappeared. Their heads hung down ; their uniforms were bloody.

"Well !" said Landon.

"He's got off, captain," groaned one; "escaped — gone !"

"Clean gone, captain !" moaned the other.

A few words conveyed the whole melancholy story. Half way to Winchester, Arden had wrested a pistol from one of his guards, wounded both of them severely, and succeeded in effecting his escape.

Landon turned to Harry Arden with a smile of grim admiration.

"Decidedly, your brother is a trump !" he said. "You ought to be proud of him !"

XXVIII.

ONE OF THE BRIGHT SPOTS IN MY MEMORY.

ON the next morning I set out from " Bizarre," and crossing the Shenandoah, by placing my saddle in a skiff, and swimming my horse, proceeded, by way of Ashby's Gap, to Fauquier, where I expected to find, and inspect, the Partisans of Mosby.

This duty I determined should be performed as soon as possible. I was anxious to return to Landon, who had evidently resolved upon some hazardous expedition. He had informed me, however, that he would remain at " Bizarre " for three or four days to rest his horses; and I promised myself that I would return, if possible, before he again moved.

I have attempted in this episode of my *memoirs* to confine myself as closely as possible to the curious events connected with the history of Landon. Were I writing a romance, indeed, " St. Leger Landon " would be an appropriate title for these pages; and, doubtless, this introduction of a central figure gives my narrative an interest more human and dramatic than could otherwise be secured. Am I wrong in so

thinking, friend? I think I am not. So I shall
not dwell upon my visit to "Mosby and his men."

At some other time I will attempt, perhaps, a
picture of those joyous Partisans, and describe their
free life amid the mountains, in the forests, or scour-
ing the great roads. It was a branch of the service
wholly different from the rest; between the Partisans
and the troops of the regular army there were few
points of resemblance, save their common courage,
their common cause, and the common enrolment of
all as soldiers of the Confederate States, fighting
under the Confederate flag.

To-day I cannot describe the Partisans, or their
lithe and "dangerous" commander, with his gray,
roving eyes, his smile, revealing the white teeth, his
brief words of command, and his daring soul.
Imagine this King of the Rangers, amid the great
forests of Fauquier, with his horse saddled near, and
his gay followers around him. Hear the jests and
laughter; see them mount and away; hear the crack
of their pistols; see the long string of blue prisoners, the "U.S." wagons, the numberless mules captured. You will say that these men are good
soldiers, who fight fairly, pistol to pistol; but read
the Northern newspapers and you will discover that
they are outlaws.

Or you would have discovered that in the good
year 1864. Now the smoke has drifted. The world

sees that these men were *soldiers!* And when their commander, Colonel Mosby, visits the Gold Room in Wall Street, some of the worthiest of his old foes shake his hand, and say, "Welcome!"

I found Mosby below Piedmont; inspected his command, which had just assembled for a raid toward Alexandria; and on the next morning set out on my return to the Valley.

I had hoped to reach the vicinity of Millwood on the same evening; but you know when you set out, you do not know when you will arrive.

Near Upperville I met my friend, Captain D——, who insisted that I should go and dine with him; and the afternoon found me still enthralled by his charming household. Then I was urged to attend a wedding festival at a neighbouring mansion, "B——;" and, yielding to the kind persistence of some irresistible personages, I went.

I wish I could describe that charming evening and that wonderful supper! Ah! my dear reader, there is a lurking vice in this life of peace; it destroys the magical effect of *contrasts*. I had been living for a long time upon about a quarter of a pound of rancid bacon and some musty meal. I had partaken of that imposing banquet from a tin plate, on the lid of a camp-chest. Worse than all, I had seen around me only gray uniforms and male human

beings. And now, as though by magic, I had entered a different world.

All around me, at the hospitable mansion of
Mrs.——, I saw bright eyes, rosy cheeks, smiling
lips, and braided hair. Round arms abounded, encircled with bracelets and draped with lace. White
necks swam in "illusion" like heaps of snowy roses,
tinted with sunset. And then the supper! — the
wondrous supper! O supper to be ever remembered! Rich viands, roasts, and stews; immense
pyramids of ice-cream; cakes, jellies, candied orange,
blanc-mange, meringues; *real* coffee! and actual
white sugar and cream!

When afterwards I described that supper to my
comrades, they smiled and nodded politely, but said
nothing. They were too polite to contradict me; but
I could see that I had made shipwreck of my character for veracity, and was regarded, in Shakespearian
phrase, as a "measureless liar!"

In truth, that was a notable spectacle on the Virginia border in 1864. Happy was the wandering
staff-officer who partook of those delicacies; happier
still in conducting the fair young bride to supper; the sweet and kindly eyes, shining under the
floating snow of the long veil and the bridal
wreath.

But no human happiness is without alloy. Suddenly a check was put to the merrymaking.

I observed a stir in the company; whispered
words passed about; the guests flowed toward the
door; and then I heard, for the first time, the hurried
words, "The Yankees are coming!"

The effect of this announcement was disagreeable.
The wedding festival was brought to an untimely
end. I returned with my fair companion to the
drawing-room, and said to an acquaintance: —

"What is the origin of the alarm?"

The old gentleman whom I addressed, and who
was busily looking for his hat, laughed and hurriedly
replied: —

"Some of Mosby's men report that the Yankees
are rapidly advancing from Middleburg. They are
expected at Upperville in half an hour. You soldiers had better get away from here!"

And he hastened to the door. The alarm had
now become general, and the guests were rolling off
in their vehicles, or hastily cantering homeward on
their horses.

I came last, with my friend Captain D——, having made my bow to the bride, and received a pressure of the small white hand, and a bright smile
which lit up the rosy face like sunshine.

Pardon my poor compliment, madam; and the
roses which bloomed that night, — may they never
fade, or turn to lilies!

Riding back to my friend's mansion, between Upperville and Middleburg, I declined his invitation to remain all night, and, resuming my arms, which I had left there, turned the head of my horse once more toward Ashby's Gap.

XXIX.

BLOUNT'S SECRET.

IT was two in the morning, and I never saw a darker night. The hoof-strokes of my horse on the turnpike sounded weird and ghostly. I must have resembled a phantom horseman traversing a world of silence.

An hour afterwards, travelling leisurely, I passed through the quiet and apparently deserted village of Paris, where not even a yelping cur greeted me, and slowly continued my way up the mountain.

All at once, as I reached the summit, near the "Big Poplar," a shadow detached itself from the tree, and, advancing rapidly, took the shape of a mounted man, pistol in hand.

"Halt! Who goes there?" said the shadow.

"A friend; that is to say, if you are a friend of The South," I replied.

"Advance, friend; you answer straight out."

"Because I know that there are no Yankees about here. I am Colonel Surry, of General Lee's army. What command is yours?"

"Captain Blount's, colonel."

" I know him, — and am glad I know him. Where is he ? "

" Here, colonel."

And a second shadow — this time on foot — came out from beneath the " Big Poplar." I had already recognized Blount.

" Dismount, and come and rest yourself," he said, pressing my hand, and speaking in his deep, sad voice ; " you ride late, my dear colonel, and must be tired. Come."

" Willingly, my dear captain," I said.

And, dismounting, I walked toward the poplar. Blount had taken the bridle of my horse, and now tethered him to a bough. A moment afterwards we were seated beside a glimmering picket-fire. No other human being was visible.

" You seem to be keeping ' lonely watch ' to-night, captain," I said, with a smile. " Where is your command ? "

" Oh ! not far," he said ; " they are sleeping yonder in that clump of trees. I will not move until sunrise."

" You are going — "

" On an expedition toward Berryville ; and I don't wish to make the attack I intend until to-morrow night. So I am not in a hurry."

" I see. I am very glad I have met you."

" Thanks, colonel."

And Blount inclined with sad but exquisite courtesy. A tongue of flame had caught a bundle of twigs near, and, by the light streaming up, I could see the calm, noble face, the graceful figure, in its close-fitting gray uniform ; the cavalry-boots fitting to the high and aristocratic instep, and the light sabre balancing the revolver. Under the brown hat with its gold cord shone the grave, soft eyes, and I could see the sad smile plainly. It was hard to realize that this man was one of those iron souls who shrink from nothing.

We entered into conversation, for I was not sleepy, and my companion seemed not to need rest. A few words explained my errand to Fauquier, and described the wedding party.

Blount remained silent for a moment.

"I have heard no firing toward Upperville," he said, at length, "and it is probable that the enemy have not come that high up. It is a pity the wedding party should have been interrupted,—a great pity."

"You say that," I said, smiling, "as if you remembered your own, and sympathized with Mr. and Mrs. —— "

Blount's head sank.

"I have never been married," he said. " No, no, colonel, — that has been spared me."

"Spared you ! Pardon me, but the future would

seem to indicate a very great indisposition to matrimony."

"It expresses my sentiment."

"You do not covet 'connubial felicity,' then, as the poets call it. Or perhaps you do not admire the female sex."

"They have worked my greatest woe, colonel."

"Women?"

"One, at least."

The words were uttered in a tone of the profoundest sadness. For some moments I said nothing. Then, thinking of the true face which had shone upon me in Winchester: —

"Oh! you do them injustice," I said; "these poor women, so much maligned, captain. They are thoughtless, they are capricious, but they are pure gold under all."

Something stern and bitter came to the face of Blount.

"I am glad your experience is such, colonel. It has not been mine," he said.

"You are a woman-hater, then?"

"No; I do not hate them. My sentiment is different."

I bowed my head, and could only murmur: —

"Something has wounded you deeply, and makes you commit a terrible injustice, captain."

Blount's eye flashed.

"An injustice, colonel! No, I am just. I am not a stern or unkind person; I would cut off my right hand before I would wrong a human being; but do not ask me to have any respect for women."

He paused and his flushed face was both sad and lowering.

"I surprise you," he said, "but my life has been sorrowful. I am not fond of confidences, colonel, but something in you wins it. Hear me say a few words, then. Suppose yourself young and unsuspecting, — suppose you love a young girl who appears the soul of truth and honour, — suppose she plights you her troth, looks at you with eyes swimming in tears of tenderness, tells you a thousand times that you are dearer to her than the very life-blood of her heart, and then betrays you, deceives you, shipwrecks your life! Suppose that! and then say if the betrayed person can respect women?"

For a moment I could not reply. Blount's tones were terrible.

"That is a romance you relate," I murmured.

"It is the truth," he replied. "Antoinette Du —— Pshaw! here I am giving real names! Let us speak of something else, colonel. This moves me beyond my wont."

And, passing his hand over his brow, Blount seemed to clear away all the mists of rising anger which had obscured his sight.

"I didn't intend to say so much, colonel," he went on sadly; "and I trust you will pardon me. These old wounds will reopen sometimes. Look upon all this as 'a romance'!"—your word,—and let us speak of other things."

"Well, captain, but your words cause me unaffected sorrow."

"That is my mood habitually, colonel," he said, smiling. "I am not gay, and least of all to-night."

"Something troubles you."

"I have a presentiment."

"A presentiment?"

Blount laughed; but his laugh was not gay.

"That I am going to die."

"Pshaw! banish all these chimeras, captain. God does not forewarn men. He strikes them when their hour comes, and they fall. Let us be ready, but not fearful."

Blount's face became calm, his eyes full of a sweet and grave kindness.

"You are right, friend," he said, "and I thank you for these words. I try to do my duty and leave the rest to my Creator. I sin against him often. I am ashamed of it, and try to reform. The enemy drove me yonder lately in a fight near the river, and I was so enraged at their running before the young ladies who had come out on the lawn, that I cursed and swore at them like a vulgar fellow.

On the next day I was ashamed, and went and begged the young ladies to pardon me. I have already asked pardon of God, colonel, and hope he will forgive everything, for I am going to die soon. Now let us not talk further of that. Tell me of Petersburg, the chance there, and what you think of the war?"

Blount evidently desired to change the subject, and we accordingly spoke of public events. Half an hour afterwards we were asleep, lying wrapped in our capes by the camp-fire.

At sunrise the troop was moving, and I parted with Blount at the river, where we swam our horses,— he proceeding down the left bank, I toward "Bizarre."

His last words to me, were: "Forget my foolish talk last night, colonel! but I will remember *your* words."

"My words?" I said.

"As to the fates of men, '*He strikes them when their hour comes, and they fall. Let us be ready, but not fearful.*'"

A grave, sweet smile accompanied the words, and, waving his hand with exquisite grace and courtesy, Blount disappeared at the head of his troop in the forest.

Half an hour afterwards I was at "*Bizarre,*" and had exchanged a close pressure of the hand with Landon.

XXX.

I HAD returned within the time; and the reader will not fail to comprehend the grounds of my anxiety to see " *Bizarre* " again.

Landon's narrative had produced a profound impression upon me. This young Virginian, so bitter and cynical at twenty-five, and pursuing with so much ardour his private vengeance, attracted me irresistibly, and I experienced an uncontrollable desire to see him again, and be present at that *denouement* of his affair with Ratcliffe, which, something told me, would not long be delayed.

The main attraction, however, was Landon himself. He had powerfully aroused my sympathy. This life darkened in its dawn; this love and friendship both betrayed; those friends turning coldly from the young man, who, thus wounded mortally in his pride and his heart, had permitted the venom of misanthropy to filtrate, drop by drop, into his blood, — all this made up an absorbing spectacle.

" Bah ! nothing that is mean is fanciful in human nature ! "

Those words had expressed all. Stern moralists might have shaken their heads and muttered " Monster! " For my part, I sighed and felt a strong sympathy for the monster!

On reaching " Bizarre," I was cordially greeted, as I have said, by Landon, who informed me that I had arrived just in time, as he was going to set out, on the next morning, on a scout toward Berryville.

" After Ratcliffe ? "

" Always," he replied, coolly. " He is at work again, and this time is burning houses over the heads of women and children."

" Your scouts keep you well informed, I suppose ? "

" Yes, especially Touch-and-go. By-the-by, that is a remarkable person, colonel. Have you noticed him ? "

" Two or three times, and he appears to be a character."

" A very curious one. He seems to have a private account to settle with the enemy."

" You do not know his history ? "

" I am wholly ignorant of it, and can only tell you that he is a perfect tiger in presence of the blue people. He seems to have dedicated his life to the work of killing as many of them as possible, and his ' account ' is kept in a decidedly original fashion."

" His ' account ' ? "

"I mean of the men he kills. He keeps a string, ties a knot in it whenever he kills an opponent, and I assure you it is already a knotty affair."

Landon had scarcely uttered the words when the door opened, and Touch-and-go came in silently, saluting as he did so. His boyish face wore its habitual expression of mildness; his voice, as he saluted Landon, was low and soft; in his hand he carried the string referred to; and as he entered he was tying a knot in it.

All at once I remembered seeing him perform that operation twice before: the first time on the night of our attack at the Chapel, just after he had shot the vidette, and again on the day when Ratcliffe was captured, when he had dashed out the brains of the picket at the gate with his own carbine.

Touch-and-go was evidently "settling his account" very steadily, for the string was nearly full of knots. To the number, as I have said, he had just added a new one, after which he quietly restored the string to his pocket, and made his report to Landon. He had penetrated the Federal lines, visited Sheridan's headquarters, seen houses burning in every direction, and observed every indication of some important movement on the part of the enemy.

"Good!" said Landon, "I think they are going to attack Early at last."

Touch-and-go waited silently to be addressed.

" Anything further, captain ? " he said at length.

" Nothing ; be ready to move with me at dawn."

Touch-and-go saluted, and was stealthily retiring, when I said : —

" You killed a man this evening, — did you not ? "

" Yes, colonel," he replied, quietly, " near Berryville. I shot him through the heart."

" That is another knot in your string."

" Yes, colonel."

" Another item in your account settled."

" I see the captain has been talking about me, colonel."

" Yes, but he does not know your history. Is it a mystery, Touch-and-go ? If not, it would interest me."

" It is no mystery, colonel. My old father and mother were burnt out by Hunter's people, on a cold and rainy night last spring. They were all night exposed without shelter, and crouching in a fence corner, to the storm ; and a month afterwards they were dead from typhoid fever. I was in the army at the time, but got off long enough to see them buried decently. Since then I have been alone in the world, and have been trying to kill as many Yankees as I can. I have killed forty-eight that I know of. Before I am killed myself I hope to make it a hundred."

I looked at the boy who uttered these words, full of calmness and simplicity.

" Do you expect to be killed, Touch-and-go ? " I asked.

" Yes, colonel. The war is getting to be a bloody affair. I think we will all be killed — if we do our duty."

" You are right," I said.

" I try to do mine, colonel, and I believe it is to kill Yankees. Forty-eight is not many; I wish it was ten thousand. But I hope to make it a hundred."

And waiting an instant to ascertain if Landon had any additional orders, the boy saluted modestly, and quietly left the apartment.

" What a war ! " I said, as the youth disappeared ; " the very children are desperate, and this one seems perfectly fearless."

" I think he never experienced the emotion," Landon replied; "and he is as pious as he seems blood-thirsty. He never utters an oath, reads his Bible, says his prayers, and is a model of sweet temper and kindness."

As Landon spoke, a knock came at the door, and one of the men entered.

" Here is a deserter, captain," he said, saluting; " he says he belongs to Captain Ratcliffe's command, and must see you."

" To Ratcliffe's ? "

" He was his orderly, he says."

" Send him in," said Landon, " and be ready with a rope there to hang him ! "

The man saluted and left the apartment. I gazed at Landon with some astonishment.

" To hang him ! " I exclaimed, as the door closed. Landon nodded.

" I see you are not familiar with the devices of our blue friends in this region, colonel. Civilized warfare is too tame for them ; they improve upon it. To wear blue coats and fight fairly is too stupid ; so they dress whole companies of ' Jesse Scouts ' in Confederate gray to deceive us."

" But — "

" This deserter ? He is sent, ten to one, by Ratcliffe. You have had a specimen of that worthy's courage ; you have here, probably, a specimen of his *finesse.* He despairs doubtless of whipping me ; he aims at entrapping me. His orderly deserts to me, discovers my numbers, halting-places, everything ; then slips off some night, returns to Ratcliffe, and before morning I am surprised, attacked, and cut to pieces, five against one, without warning, all in consequence of having listened with confiding simplicity to his emissary."

" You are right."

" I think so. The trick is stale and will not fool me."

" You will hang this boy ? "

" Is he a boy ? "

" Yes ; I saw him that night at Chapeldale, and he brought Ratcliffe's detachment in pursuit."

" Well, you see he is the confidential orderly, emissary, spy of his master. My rope is going to be put in requisition in twenty minutes."

As he spoke, the door opened and the deserter was ushered in.

XXXI.

THE DESERTER.

IT was, in fact, the young orderly who had fired upon me that night at Chapeldale, and then mounted and escaped. I saw before me the same brilliant black eyes; the same mocking smile on the red lips; the same rosy cheeks and rounded outlines.

The youth was clad in a handsome uniform, consisting of ample blue pantaloons, falling over small and delicate boots; a full roundabout with bright buttons, and dazzling *chevrons* on the sleeves; a light waistcoat, fitting closely to the figure; and over the broad white brow, edged with short auburn curls, fell the ample rim of a blue cavalry hat, with a golden cord around it.

Such was the costume of the boy, — half private's, half officer's. It was his mode of wearing it, however, which attracted most attention. Never did costume sit more jauntily upon human being; never had I realized so completely the gay *vivandière* of the French comedy. Everything about the boy was feminine and coquettish; no other words convey the idea. And, as the reader will soon perceive, there was the best reason in the world for the phenomenon in question.

The young deserter advanced straight into the apartment, and distributed a comprehensive smile, which had in it something decidedly satirical. Instead of being abashed, he appeared completely at his ease, and returned Landon's cold glance with a *sang froid* which was incomprehensible.

"Who are you?" said the Partisan, coldly.

"A deserter at your service; from Captain Ratcliffe's company," was the reply.

The voice was low and musical; the accent decidedly French.

"Your name?" continued Landon, as coldly as before.

The deserter looked around. On his lips the mocking smile grew more defined.

"Would you like to know?"

"Since I ask you, —speak!"

"Dismiss that man."

And the boy pointed coolly to the guard standing behind him.

"Good!" said Landon; "the comedy grows decidedly amusing. You dictate orders at my headquarters; but no matter."

And with a movement of his hand he dismissed the guard, who went out, closing the door behind him.

" Now, request this gentleman to retire in his turn."

" Speak in his presence," said Landon.

The deserter looked fixedly at the Partisan.

" I may speak before him of your most private affairs ? "

" My *private* affairs ! You ? Yes; they are all known to him."

" Very good," was the cool answer. " First you asked my name, I think ? "

" Yes."

" My name is Antoinette Duvarny."

And the speaker calmly sat down in an arm-chair opposite Landon.

At the words " My name is Antoinette Duvarny " I could not suppress a start. The words of Blount suddenly returned to my memory. " Antoinette Du — pshaw ! here I am giving real names. " Could the person before me be a woman, — and by any possibility that woman of whom Blount had spoken ? Had this singular " deserter " played the main part in that tragic drama which had overshadowed the life of so brave and noble a gentleman ? The fact seemed incredible; but there was the astonishing similarity of name. " Antoinette Du— " could be no one beside " Antoinette Duvarny," I said to myself.

I was thus reflecting, when the woman resumed,

with a laugh, which displayed a set of pearly teeth,
"My sex gives me permission to drop ceremony, my
dear Captain Landon, and I am sure that such a
gallant gentleman as yourself would never keep a
lady standing."

Landon was gazing at her keenly.

"Then you are a woman?" he said.

"At your service."

"Your object in deserting?"

"To reach *you.*"

"Why?"

The deserter smiled.

"To betray you, of course. Are they not preparing the rope yonder to hang me as soon as our
little talk is over?"

"That was not your design, then?"

The deserter shrugged her shoulders.

"No; something very different."

"Speak plainly."

"With pleasure. Well, in coming to make you
a visit, my dear Captain Landon, I am prompted by
a sentiment which is said to be powerful with women
when it gains possession of them, — the sentiment,
namely, of vengeance."

"Vengeance?"

"Precisely; and upon one whom I hate bitterly, — a dear common friend of ours."

Landon was silent, gazing at the speaker. His

13

glance seemed piercing enough to penetrate her soul.

" You mean Captain Ratcliffe ? "

" Yes."

" You hate him? "

" For the last month, bitterly."

" You would avenge some wrong upon him ? "

" Yes, by telling you, his enemy, what will send you on his track; make you hunt him day and night; keep you from eating, drinking, sleeping, until you have his blood."

A flash darted from the black eyes. It was easy to see that there was not the least acting in this person. Never was hatred more clearly expressed in mortal face.

Landon's cheeks filled with blood; his eyes glowed.

" Speak ! " he said, in an imperious voice. " I am listening."

And his dark eyes were riveted upon the countenance of the deserter.

XXXII.

THE deserter greeted Landon's threatening glance and address with perfect nonchalance.

"A moment," she said, stretching out carelessly a small foot in the most delicate boot imaginable. "Monsieur seems really about to eat me! Fie! that is not gallant to a lady."

Landon leaned his elbow upon the table beside him, rested his forehead upon his hand, and awaited in gloomy silence.

"*Eh bien!*" said the deserter, in her satirical voice; "that is better. You are more reasonable, my dear Captain Landon. I see that you have made up your mind to listen to my highly interesting communication without interruption; and I assure you that there are certain portions of it which will tax your self-control to the utmost."

Landon made no reply; he listened. The deserter continued : —

"I have referred to Ratcliffe as your enemy. What if I tell you that *I* have been an enemy a thousand times more deadly, — though inspired by no rancour at all toward *you?* Such is the fact, Captain Landon. I come here in the midst of your 'Night Hawks,' where your will is law, to tell you that; and I do so because I know you to be a brave man and a gentleman, — not the base, petty tyrant I have left yonder.

"Listen, sir," continued the deserter, with a bitter smile, — "listen, and I will relate a very curious series of events for your entertainment. They would interest the most indifferent, for I swear to you they are singular; they will interest, above all, Captain St. Leger Landon, for they explain how Miss Adair came to break his heart."

"Miss Adair!"

"And her own nearly, at the same moment," added the deserter.

Landon shuddered. In his white face his eyes resembled two red hot coals.

"Speak!" he muttered, hoarsely.

"You will not interrupt me?"

"I will not."

"Then listen," continued the deserter, coolly, "and I will tell you everything. My object in revealing all this will appear later.

"Let us go back, if you please, Monsieur Landon, to the year 1860, at which time you and this dear Ratcliffe were fellow-students at West Point, and I was residing in a village not far distant. I

was not, however, a native of the North. I was
born in New Orleans, where I first met the charming Ratcliffe; and — shall I tell you everything?
— relate a little romance for your amusement?
You will scarcely understand, unless I begin at the
beginning."

"Proceed," said Landon, in a low voice.

"With great pleasure," said the deserter, with a
singular smile.

And in tones of bitter humour she resumed : —

"My story will not be long. I was born of
French parents, in the city of New Orleans, and at
a ball one evening met a young Mr. Ratcliffe, from
East Tennessee. He was exceedingly handsome,
and paid me marked attention. On the next day he
called to see me; and, to be brief, became, or pro-
fessed to be, romantically enamoured of my dear
self. I was flattered, — my suitor was an Adonis,
you see, Monsieur Landon, — and I listened to his
flattering protestations. I should not have done so,
for I had already plighted my word to a gentleman
a thousand times more worthy of respect and love
than this person Ratcliffe. I was thus guilty of a
base wrong to Mr. ——; but I will not soil his
name by pronouncing it with my lips. I will only
say that I was the affianced of one immeasurably
superior to this Tennessee Adonis; and that I de-

ceived and betrayed him, breaking his heart for the
love of a vulgar *poltroon!*

"Well, things took their course. Ratcliffe continued his addresses secretly, and proposed that we
should be married secretly, as the rage of Mr. ——
—that is, of my affianced — would be great. That
should have opened my eyes ; but I was foolishly in
love with the Tennesseean, and I consented. We
were accordingly married privately. I left my family
with only a few lines of adieu; went to Tennessee
with Ratcliffe ; and thence accompanied him to West
Point, in a village near which place I took up my
residence. Here he visited me regularly, by leaving
West Point without permission ; and I went more
than once to see him at his own quarters. At his
quarters ! you may exclaim, — a woman visit a West
Point Cadet at his quarters ? Yes, my dear Captain Landon, nothing in this wicked world is more
deceiving than 'appearances.' Is not life a comedy,
or a tragedy, at best ? Are not the costumes half
the spectacle ? The dress, does not that make the
man or the woman ? Well, I observed that a *cadet*
was a human being in a little swallow-tailed coat,
striped pantaloons, and a cap of peculiar fashion ;
and as my dear Ratcliffe brought me a uniform, I
became a 'West Point Cadet' in ten minutes. I
enjoyed the frolic, for there has always been a spice
of *diablerie* in my character. I dressed myself, and

looked with admiration at my figure. In my jaunty
little uniform, with my hair hidden beneath the cap,
and walking arm in arm with Ratcliffe, it was impossible to mistake me for anything but a military
youth; and the proof is, that you saw me a dozen
times, and we were once introduced; you never
suspected me!

"Well, this is growing tedious — to proceed to
events. In speaking of what took place in New
Orleans, I was somewhat inaccurate. I stated that
Ratcliffe and myself were 'married.' I should have
said that I believed at the time that we were married
lawfully; the real fact, however, was, that this dear
Ratcliffe had tricked and betrayed me. I was poor.
Ratcliffe discovered that, and he deceived me by a
sham marriage. One of his companions personated
a priest, — the whole ceremony was a farce, — and I
only came to know this months afterwards, when in
the North. Ratcliffe taunted me with the fact one
day, when he was shamefully intoxicated, and when
something between us had led to hot words.

"I will not stop to describe my feelings at this
announcement. I think it aroused the devil in me;
and Ratcliffe afterwards told me that the very expression of my eyes sobered him; they 'looked like
red hot coals,' he was pleased to say; and, indeed, I
could have killed him at that moment, or put an end
to myself. This, then, was the man for whom I had

betrayed — my affianced, his superior a million times! For this vulgar wretch I had broken the noblest heart I have ever known! Well, an hour afterwards I had grown calm. Ratcliffe had soothed and again deceived me. I was foolishly in love with his pretty face, and again trusted him. He had deceived me, he acknowledged; but with no intention to do so really. His family would never have consented to the match, he said; but he would soon be his own master; he would wed me before the whole world; and I was lulled to sleep again.

"Charming evidences of my dear Ratcliffe's confidence followed this *désagrément*," continued the deserter, satirically. "He was more confiding than ever before, less reserved as to his past life; and so one day he related a curious incident, which I think will interest *you*, Captain Landon, since it refers to a certain Miss Adair of this neighbourhood."

Landon's face slightly flushed. Otherwise he remained unmoved.

"Continue," he said, coolly.

"With pleasure," the deserter replied. "Well, the incident related by my dear Ratcliffe was this. He informed me that just before meeting me he had made the acquaintance of a young lady in Virginia; had paid his addresses to her; she had led him on step by step; then when he spoke, she had laughed at him, refusing his suit with hauteur and positive

insult. When I asked if it was possible that
'such deception could be practised by any one,'
Ratcliffe growled out for reply, that he had been
betrayed by a rival. The young lady had fallen
crazily in love with a certain St. Leger Landon;
Landon was his friend; the very confidence reposed
in you had been his, Ratcliffe's, destruction; he
would be revenged on you and the young lady!

"He told me all this with flashing eyes, and a
face red with violent anger. He had long ceased to
care for Miss Adair, he added, but he would give his
right hand to be revenged upon her and the treacher-
ous friend, who, knowing his passion for her, had
basely interposed, and, by his deceitful arts, won the
heart of the young lady from him!

"When he spoke thus, I laughed; and probably
with a bitter sneer in the laughter.

"'What are you laughing at?' said Ratcliffe.

"'At your ideas of "baseness" and "deceitful
arts,"' I said. 'That is the way you won me.'

"His face grew black; but, seeing that this expression did not intimidate me in the least, he con-
trolled his anger, assumed a wheedling tone, and
resumed his narrative. A few additional words terminated it. What he now had resolved on, he said,
was full vengeance. Would I assist him? If I
consented, he would marry me at once! Only to
secure his vengeance!

"I have never seen *hate* expressed so strongly. He positively magnetized me — this dear Ratcliffe! He was extremely handsome, and his anger became him. Then his proposal was not so disagreeable. To strike *my* rival did not positively revolt me! To be brief, Ratcliffe saw that he had made the desired impression, and proceeded at once to lay before me the scheme which he had devised.

"Shall I go on, sir, or do I weary you? But no reply to that question is necessary. I see from your countenance, Captain Landon, that you are by no means weary. Well, to proceed with my story. Ratcliffe may be base, — *I* have never seen any one more so, — but after hearing me to the end, you will be compelled to confess that he is ingenious!"

XXXIII.

THE RING.

With the same subtle and mocking smile upon the lips, the deserter continued : —

"Ratcliffe's plan was excellent, and had the simplicity of genius. I need not tell you, my dear Captain Landon, that cunning is more dangerous in this world than force; that the most deadly of all weapons, the keenest-edged tools to play with, are the passions of the human heart !

"Well, our dear Ratcliffe determined to play upon the love existing between yourself and Miss Adair. His object, he declared, was to ruin your character, break your engagement, destroy your 'insolent happiness,' — I well remember that phrase, — and so 'get even' with you and the young lady at the same moment. In this he required my assistance, — would I give it ? If I would aid him he would repay me by wedding me at once. We would return to Tennessee, whence he came, and live in wealth and luxury. Such was his offer, and it won me. Do you laugh at me ? Well, I deserve it. But, to be frank again, I was very much in love with this poor wretch at the time. His superb face and figure had impressed my foolish fancy. I listened, assented; three days afterward I had basely acted as he dictated.

"You shall judge if I am wrong in saying that I acted basely. Ratcliffe had said to me : 'The first thing was to make Landon's friends and family think him a reprobate and a blackguard. I have seen to that, he is ruined; now, the next thing is to destroy him in the estimation of the girl he loves. Here is a ring and a draft of a letter: copy and sign the letter, enclose the ring in it, and put the whole in this envelope.' With these words he left me, and I read the rough draft of the letter. It was truly devilish ! — and I copied and sent it to Miss Adair; sent the ring with it also, — your *engagement ring*, which Ratcliffe afterward acknowledged he had drawn from your finger while you were asleep ! "

Landon had listened, pale and cold, but his face now flushed.

"I remember missing the ring," he muttered, "but thought that I had lost it while bathing in the Hudson."

"No, it was stolen from you; you know, at last, how, and by whom."

"And that letter," said Landon, in an altered

voice, — a voice full of inexpressible menace, —
"what was that letter?"

"Would you like to hear me repeat it? But, no,
that is not necessary. In the graceful little docu-
ment, Mademoiselle Antoinette Duvarny presented
her compliments to Miss Ellen Adair, and begged to
return to that young lady the engagement ring
which she had given to Mr. St. Leger Landon, and
which Mr. St. Leger Landon had in turn presented
to Mademoiselle Duvarny."

Landon half rose ; his eyes blazed.

"You were base enough to do that!" he said,
hoarsely, his brow wet with cold perspiration.

"Yes," was the cool reply.

"And you dare to confess it! confess it to me!
— Miserable wretch — "

And Landon's hand was extended as though to
clutch some weapon.

"It was necessary," came as coolly. "I would
have concealed this, but could not. For the rest,
Captain Landon, I am not compelled to speak. If
you do not wish to know all, tell me so, and I will
say no more."

"Go on," came in the same hoarse tone.

"Very good — to continue."

And the deserter went on in a voice in which it
was impossible to discern the least emotion.

"I was speaking of the engagement ring which

Mademoiselle Duvarny begged to return to Miss
Adair, its original owner. Mr. Landon — the letter
said — had for some time been *the lover* of Miss
Duvarny; in the confidence of private intercourse
had mentioned his little affair of the past with Miss
Adair; had laughed at it; spoken slightingly of Miss
A.; declared himself weary of the affair completely;
and had given her, Miss Duvarny, the little token
which she now returned, since she was unwilling to
retain the property of Miss Adair, *under the peculiar circumstances.*

"That was all. But it was quite enough, — was
it not? A month afterwards Ratcliffe came to me
gleefully, and informed me that he had received intelligence that your engagement with Miss Adair
had terminated. I never saw him more joyful.

"'That was a master-stroke!' he said, 'and I
knew it would succeed, for I defy any *woman* to act
differently under the same circumstances. Acknowledge, my dear,' he went on, 'that the thing
was a real thunderbolt! You write on your pretty
little note-paper the history of your little affair with
our friend Landon; you enclose his *engagement
ring* given you by him, — what woman, after that,
but would scorn to see his face again, as long as she
lived?'

"'True,' I replied, 'it was ingenious, but I feel
like the base woman I am, for the part I had in it.

Nevertheless, it is done, and now give me my reward.'

" 'Your reward?' he asked.

" 'Yes,' I replied; 'marry me and take me to Tennessee. — I am tired of this.'

" His reply was a laugh.

" 'Did I think he was in earnest?'

" I could have strangled him, and I think my hatred commenced from that very moment. He continued to reply to all my entreaties with the same laughter; said only that some day, *perhaps*, he would keep his promise; and then, in the midst of all this, the war broke out. Ratcliffe was assigned to duty with the army in Missouri, — came to tell me good-by, and set out to join his command. I was basely deserted.

" Well, two weeks afterwards I rejoined him, wearing the dress of a boy. I continued with him; came hither with him, loving him foolishly, blindly, — a pleasing confession, is it not, gentlemen? I continued to fill my post of orderly to Ratcliffe, with my feelings unchanged, until — he met and again began to love Miss Adair!"

The speaker paused. Her voice changed. She had spoken up to this moment in a careless and mocking tone, but, as she uttered those words, "until he met and again began to love Miss Adair," her accent became cold and menacing.

"My story is nearly finished," she added, with a threatening flash of the eye, "and a few words will tell you what has happened recently. Then I will come to the main point,—my errand here!"

XXXIV.

THE OFFER AND REFUSAL.

"RATCLIFFE went to see Miss Adair," continued the deserter, "on the day after his arrival in the neighbourhood.

"He commanded a full company of regular cavalry; established his camp in the vicinity of the young lady's residence; and, taking a guard of a dozen men, went to visit her. I think he was afraid of guerillas. He is not a coward, but he is not brave. Well, he went, and I went with him, anxious to see the face of the woman whom he had *once loved*.

"It was a very beautiful face. More still, — it was pure and high-bred. This was a *lady* truly. Well, Ratcliffe's manner to Miss Adair, who received him with freezing coldness, was the perfection of laughing carelessness; you would have sworn that he cared nothing for her. They were old acquaintances, he said; the war had wafted him hither; he thought he would call and see her, as well as Judge Adair; and, if he could be of use to them in any way, they had only to indicate it.

"'These polite speeches, however, made not the least impression. I was standing at the door, and saw Judge Adair's eye flash; as to the young lady, she was a veritable iceberg; and Ratcliffe came out and rode off in a towering rage at his reception.

"That did not prevent him, however, from going again; and again I accompanied him as his orderly, and witnessed his reception. More, — I heard the conversation between himself and Miss Adair, her father being ill; and this conversation related to yourself, Captain Landon. Ratcliffe spoke of the time before the war, when he was a guest in your house at 'Bizarre,' and something had occurred there, it seemed, slightly differing from the statement which he had made to me at West Point. In other words, it was *Ratcliffe* who had tried to steal away Miss Adair's affection from *you*, — to break your engagement, while he was residing in your house as your guest; and this fact Miss Adair now referred to, and charged him with. He laughed, but far from gayly. It sounded like a growl rather, — that harsh and forced laughter. He replied that the charge was true; 'but Landon's character had justified him.' You were a 'sneak and a coward, as was proved by your leaving the country and giving up the woman you loved for a mere fancy.' She turned pale as he spoke; her eyes — they are grand eyes! — flashed haughtily. 'He is not here!' she said,

superbly, 'it is easy to see that you know that,
sir!' Half an hour afterwards Ratcliffe left her,
white with rage, gnawing his lips, muttering curses,
and — *loving her!*

" I saw that, and it raised the demon in me. For
this man had subjected my whole life to his will. I
had despised myself, struggled against my infatuation, sought to break the chain that bound me; but
without success. I loved him still, and up to that
moment was his slave. But at the moment when I
discovered that he loved Miss Adair, I began to feel
my free will return to me. Revenge began to replace love. Not revenge upon *her*, — for she had
done nothing; she despised this man, — but on *him*.

" Events hastened. Going everywhere with Ratcliffe, I was at the ford yonder when you attacked
and drove him back upon Millwood. I bore him off
that night when you had bruised him by a blow of your
pistol, from which he soon recovered, however. I
was at the Chapel with him, where he was not engaged, and afterwards went with him to Miss Adair's,
where you, sir," — and the speaker turned to me, —
" captured the valiant Ratcliffe and carried him off.
Well, on that night I yielded to a weak impulse and
brought up the cavalry which recaptured him. I
was repaid by another scene that night at Judge
Adair's, in which he stormed at, insulted, and declared his love for Miss Adair. Then you captured

him in turn, Captain Landon; he escaped, and another visit, still, to Miss Adair, followed.

"Let me finish. For the last three days his infatuation has become a species of madness. He has repulsed, insulted, spurned, put his heel upon me! I am no longer anything but the wretched slave of his caprice! He has made nothing of telling me that I am disgusting in his eyes. He has dared to use a term in addressing me that I will not repeat! Yes, this man, to whom I have sacrificed everything, — for whom I have lost name and fame, and all that a woman values, — this base, cowardly wretch, who has lied and tricked and betrayed others for so long, has now insulted, outraged, and betrayed *me!*

"He has betrayed me!" continued the speaker, with flaming eyes; "but woe to him! He has not counted on the Basque blood of the Duvarnys! I have but one aim, — to crush him! And now, perhaps, you understand why I have come hither, Captain Landon. I come to say, You have only to follow me to surprise and destroy the bitterest enemy you have in the world! I will lead you straight to him; will deliver him into your hands, asking one thing only, — that you will allow me to be present when you bury your sword in his cowardly heart!"

She paused, shuddering with rage. It was an absorbing spectacle, — that beautiful face convulsed; that bosom shaken by wrath; those lips half open, and showing the white teeth close-set beneath.

"Will you follow me?" she said, hoarsely and abruptly to Landon; "I will go unarmed between two men; you can shoot me if I betray you; will you follow me?"

"No!" said Landon, rising.

"You refuse!"

"I will do better," said the Partisan, coldly. "I will kill him in fair fight before your eyes, or he shall kill me!"

XXXV.

IN THE "FOX-SPRING WOODS."

I HAVE said that in returning from Fauquier to the Valley, I had hastened my steps, in order to be present at the *denouement* of the affair between Landon and Ratcliffe, — a *denouement* which something told me would not long be delayed.

That "something" was the intense bitterness of the adversaries; the knowledge upon Landon's part that his enemy had destroyed his character, and the fact that *Ratcliffe doubtless knew that he knew it.* That was enough to make two men thirst for each other's blood; but now a far more bitter sentiment of hatred inflamed Landon; and I foresaw an early termination of the drama.

Ratcliffe had not only blackened his good name; he had produced that rupture with Miss Adair which had nearly broken Landon's heart. It was easy to understand that from this moment the young Partisan would never rest; that he would follow Ratcliffe as a bloodhound follows the trail. When they met, one would die.

It was this fierce wrestle which I now looked for-

214

ward to with absorbing interest. On the day after
the interview which I have just described, Landon
was in the saddle at the head of about thirty men,
and we were proceeding in the direction of Berryville.

The deserter had remained behind, by his order,
at "Bizarre;" but this order, as the reader will
perceive, availed little.

I shall now attempt to narrate, in their regular
order, the strangely tragic events which occurred in
the neighbourhood of the Old Chapel. I look back
to these events with a sort of wonder, asking myself
if they really took place before my eyes, or were
only a dream. Here at Eagle's Nest, in 1868, all
that past looks so strange! That autumn of 1864,
when I marched and fought with Landon, seems an
unreal epoch; Millwood, the Lover's Leap, Bizarre,
the Old Chapel, mere imaginary places, which I
have visited in slumber, dozing here in my elbow-
chair!

But you nestle yonder still, — do you not, — little
village of Millwood, on the banks of the limpid
stream, stealing on to the Shenandoah? Lover's
Leap! you still hang above the flowing river.
Weeping willows of the Old Chapel! you are sighing still, I think, above the graves of the dear dead
ones; the brave children of the Valley whom I loved
and will ever love! — sighing now in 1868, when

the hours are dull and long, as in 1864, when they rushed onward, crammed with adventure; when every minute sounded the death-knell of some heart that poured out its blood for Virginia!

O wondrous days and nights of 1864, on the banks of the Shenandoah! Golden days, moonlight nights of that dreamy autumn! I have seen much in my time, and have many things to remember; but I will forget all before I forget *you!*

Landon passed through Millwood at the head of his men, left the little church embowered in trees behind him, and, advancing steadily, reached a point on the Berryville road about two miles from Millwood.

Here he obliqued to the right, followed a narrow road for a few hundred yards, and then, penetrating the forest, halted his men in a hollow of what are called the " Fox-Spring Woods."

He then informed me that he was going to ride ahead, in order to reconnoitre in person, and invited me to accompany him. To this I gladly assented; and Arden, having been left in command of the Night-Hawks, Landon turned his horse's head toward the Chapel.

As we went on through the woods, advancing slowly amid the thick undergrowth, I observed upon the Partisan's countenance evidences of unwonted emotion.

"Something moves you, Landon," I said, gazing at him; "what is it?"

"It would puzzle me to tell you," was his reply.

And, riding on for a few moments in silence, he suddenly added: —

"Do you believe in presentiments?"

"Yes, and no."

"Well, I believed in them this morning!"

"You feel some presentiment? Of what? Of evil?"

"I cannot reply to that. I can only say that something tells me this day will prove an epoch in my life, — a sad life for the rest, and scarce worth an epoch!"

"Come, cheer up!"

"I am not cast down. On the contrary a strange force seems to have come to me, — my blood rushes through my veins, as if to meet and breast some struggle that is near! Something drives me on; do you remember the Greek Necessity with her iron wedge? In her hands the gods themselves were powerless!"

I looked curiously at Landon, and he caught my glance. A grim smile came to his lips.

"You are surprised at my fanciful talk," he said, "but I assure you it expresses my feelings to-day. I *know* that I am going to engage in some desperate struggle. I go to it blindly, with my feet dragged —

without free will.   As to its character or result, I
know nothing, and cannot say whether it will be
fortunate or unfortunate, — happy or terrible."

His head sank, and he went on in silence.   Then
the head rose; the face of the Partisan had assumed
an expression which I had never seen upon it before.
That expression was sweet and yet resolute;   a
strange mingling of gentleness and courage.

"I know not how it is, Surry," he said, thought-
fully;   "but all my life seemed to pass before me as
I rode on, this morning.   It is a strange life, — is it
not? and enough to account for that bitterness and
cynicism which you must have noted in me.   Sometimes I am puzzled, — I wander and stumble in my
thought, — I believe in God, in his merciful Prov-
idence, in his goodness, his justice; but at times
the devil comes, and whispers in my ear: 'You
are the victim of a blind fatality; there is no Prov-
idence; all is the sport of chance !'

"Do you wonder at that?   Think of my life !   I
was a happy and warm-hearted boy; now I am a
cold and dreary man.   I loved my mother as dearly
as man could, and she was murdered by those cowardly gossips.   I loved a woman, — and she threw
me away without hearing me say a word in my
defence.   Then this terrible war came to finish me,
and make me old.   Think of this country, in which
my youth passed so happily, laid waste with fire and

sword, — the smiling homes reduced to ashes, the brave boys in bloody graves in the Old Chapel yonder, the very grave of my mother exposed at any moment to desecration!

"Is it strange, then, that I am hard and an old man before my time? — that I doubt the goodness of God sometimes — miserable creature that I am! — and feel tempted to cry out 'Vengeance! be thou my god!' It is bitter food we eat, a bitter fountain we drink from, in this year of our Lord 1864! And what is left us, but to fight on? For my part I shall never lower my flag until the end; and a bullet, perhaps to-day, may save me that trouble."

I looked steadily at him.

"You think it will?" I said.

"Who knows? Did I not tell you just now that I felt a singular presentiment?"

"Pshaw! You did not sleep last night, Landon, you are nervous!"

He smiled grimly.

"On the contrary I slept soundly, — only I dreamed."

"What did you dream?"

"That a house was burning somewhere; that Ratcliffe met me hilt to hilt in single combat; that a rope was thrown around my feet by unseen hands; I was dragged to the ground, and Ratcliffe leaned his sword's point on my throat, when I awoke!"

"Good! Remember that dreams always go 'by contraries,' Landon. None of this is going to happen!"

"You are wrong," said Landon, coolly; "and there is the beginning!"

As he spoke, he pointed through an opening in the woods. To the left of the Old Chapel I saw a dense smoke rising. A second glance convinced me that it was Chapeldale on fire.

XXXVI.

In an instant all Landon's preoccupation had disappeared. Dreams, presentiments, memories, — all had vanished, leaving the Partisan's eye fiery, his lip firm-set, his muscle strong for the coming conflict.

Plunging the spurs into his horse, he darted forward, leaped a ravine, and gained a knoll from which the eye embraced the whole landscape.

"Chapeldale!" he said.

Suddenly the noise of hoofs resounded on the turnpike in our front. A moment afterwards, a white robe gleamed, a lady on horseback appeared; she approached at full gallop, and I recognized Miss Adair.

We spurred to meet her, and she drew rein. I have never seen acuter distress than that written upon her face.

"Captain Landon!" she exclaimed; and a sudden rush of crimson to her cheeks betrayed her deep emotion at the encounter.

Landon bowed low; I could see his heart throbbing.

"I was coming to look for help from some one. They have carried off my father."

And, unnerved, overwhelmed, the young lady burst into tears. In an instant, however, she had dashed away the tears, and her hurried words put us in possession of the main points of a scene, of which I afterward heard all the details.

Ratcliffe had come on that morning to Chapeldale with a detachment of cavalry, and, finding Judge Adair ill in bed, had demanded an interview with the young lady, who reluctantly made her appearance. Ratcliffe was pale and gloomy, and, having closed the door, informed Miss Adair that he had come to visit her for the last time. He had sworn, he declared, to attain the object which he had so long sought, and Miss Adair was perfectly aware of the subject to which he alluded.

When she demanded an explanation, declaring herself at a loss to comprehend him, Ratcliffe brutally announced that his object was to force her into a union with him. The war was nearly over, he said; the people of the Valley utterly impoverished; *he* was rich from speculation, and he came to offer the young lady his hand and his fortune. If she consented, they would live wherever she wished; he would resign his commission, go to Paris, obey her slightest caprice. If she refused, — then he had made up his mind. He would drag her sick father from his bed, set fire to the house, and carry the old man off to take his chance of living or dying from exposure. Miss Adair might have her choice, — wealth and luxury as his wife; if she refused him, the destruction of all she held most dear. Crouching in presence of the burning roofs of Chapeldale, with her sick father carried off by his troopers before her eyes, she would then understand the love of a man like himself. He had sworn in his heart that he would do this, and would keep his oath.

Such had been Ratcliffe's announcement. Miss Adair had replied by a bitter and scornful refusal. Rather than wed him, she would die a thousand deaths, — submit to all, — and as to her father, God would watch over him.

Ratcliffe's fury at this reply passed all bounds. Raging like a wild beast, he had ordered Judge Adair to be dragged out of his bed and placed on horseback, the house to be fired, — and these orders had been promptly obeyed. Miss Adair had, meanwhile, hastened out of the house to the stable, saddled their sole remaining horse with her own hands, and, profiting by the confusion, made her escape across the fields in the direction of Millwood, where she hoped to find some of the Partisans, and lead them back to the relief of her father.

As she ascended the hill near the "Fox-Spring Woods," our gray uniforms in the foliage had attracted her attention; she had hastened to give the alarm; "if no time was lost we might be able to rescue her father."

Landon's sole reply was : —

" I hope to arrive in time."

And, raising his whistle to his lips, he sounded the cavalry signal, "Rally on the Chief."

Before five minutes had elapsed, a sudden tramping was heard in the forest; the Rangers appeared coming on at full speed; and, placing himself in front of them, with drawn sabre, Landon darted at a headlong gallop in the direction of the burning house.

XXXVII.

NO QUARTER.

THAT rush across the fields, leaping rocks, ravines, fences, was a superb spectacle, and the memory of it still stirs my blood.

We swept by to the left of the Old Chapel, crossed a meadow, mounted the Chapeldale hill, and were in front of the burning mansion, from whose windows spouted smoke and flame.

Above, a great black cloud, like the smoke rising from a gigantic torch, hovered, assumed fantastic outlines, and slowly drifted away, darkening the calm September landscape, and disappearing upon the horizon.

Landon had rushed up the hill in front of his men. His eyes blazed. I saw that the tiger was aroused in him.

"Look!" he said, with a whirl of his sabre, as he turned in his saddle and pointed to the house. "Women, children, and the sick are their victims, — and they are yonder!"

With a quick gesture he indicated a detachment of blue horsemen ascending a hill toward Berryville.

15

"No quarter!" he shouted. "Follow me!—and no quarter to-day!"

As he spoke, Landon darted on the track of the Federal cavalry. The rangers followed him headlong. From their ranks rose a wild and furious cry,—"No quarter!"

What followed seems to-day, as I go back in memory, like some terrible phantasmagoria,—some nightmare of blood and death rather than an actual occurrence.

On that morning of September, I saw Partisan warfare, in its darkest and most frightful phase.

Landon's fierce rush carried him over the distance which separated him from the Federal cavalry in an incredibly brief space of time. Nothing made him pause for an instant. Riding, drawn sabre in hand, twenty yards ahead of his men, the Partisan cleared every obstacle, drove on with bloody spurs, and then I saw him,—for I had not been able to keep up with his headlong rush,—I saw him disappear in the midst of the enemy, cutting right and left with the sabre.

The Rangers followed: every man selected his adversary,—for the Federal detachment numbered scarcely more than thirty men,—and in a few minutes the blue horsemen were scattered in wild flight.

But the flight did not avail them. On their track

followed Landon and his *sabreurs*, cutting them out of the saddle, or pistolling them, man by man.

A dozen times I heard the cry "I surrender!" and saw hands thrown up, arms dropped. Each time came the terrible response : —

"No quarter!"

And the men who had surrendered, like those who still fought, were shot, sabred, or hurled from the saddle, and trampled under foot. If they rose, a pistol bullet was sent through them, or they were ridden down, and mercilessly put to death at the point of the sword.*

Of the whole command, a few only escaped; among whom, as I afterwards discovered, was Ratcliffe. The speed of his horse had alone saved him.

A mile from the Chapel toward Berryville, the affair had come to an end. The road was strewed with dead men and horses. Not a wounded man was seen. They had all been pistolled.

Landon wiped his bloody sabre on his horse's mane.

"So much for the house-burners!" he said, coolly; "I think I have done for them!"

* Fact.

XXXVIII.

"PARTISAN RANCOUR."

JUDGE ADAIR had been recaptured, and we found him awaiting us on the hill above the Chapel, his daughter on horseback beside him.

The old cavalier's weakness seemed suddenly to have left him. He sat his horse as erect as the Cid Campeador himself, his gray hairs streaming upon his shoulders, his eyes flashing with joy.

"Thanks! thanks!" he exclaimed, as the Rangers came up. And he grasped the hand of Landon, of Arden, mine, and those of the men.

"Don't mind my house," he said, looking toward Chapeldale, which was now a great mass of roaring and crackling flames; "it is nothing. I do not regret it, as you have given such a good account of the rascals who insulted me. I have plenty of friends near Millwood; they will give me a resting-place for my gray hairs, and take care of Ellen!"

And the light of a superb courage flashed grandly from the old cavalier's fiery eyes as he uttered the words.

Landon hastened, however, with his men to the

mansion, and the Rangers exerted themselves to rescue as many valuables as possible from the flames.
These were few, however. The house was a sea of
flame. Two hours afterwards the walls alone were
standing; and the hospitable mansion of Chapeldale
was a mass of blackened ruin, — a thing of the past.

Landon was sitting his horse, looking gloomily at
the ruin.

"Look," he said, "this is the way they make
war on us in the Valley. We are wild beasts to be
hunted down, and smoked out of our dens. The
torch is to accomplish what the sword cannot; they
cannot whip our soldiers; they burn out and starve
our women and children, and if we murmur we are
told that we are — rebels! Let a writer hereafter describe this scene, Surry, and he will not be
believed. 'Partisan rancour! Sectional hatred!'
the North will cry; and not one in a thousand will
credit him. But you see. Here is the terrible fact
staring you straight in the face. This country is to
be desolated, in order that our troops cannot operate
in it. 'A crow flying over the region shall be compelled to carry his rations!' they declare. Well,
they desolate the poor Valley by burning out women
and children, and, for fear that the crow may find
food, they destroy that too. Let them starve, those
women and children! Are they not rebels? See
that dangerous one!"

And Landon pointed to Miss Adair, who was leaning on the shoulder of her old negro mammy, and trying to stifle her sobs. Beside her stood Judge Adair, still erect and defiant.

"They are right!" said Landon; "there is only one way to conquer such a race as that, — it is to starve or exterminate them!"

They were starved, reader. Ask the Army of Northern Virginia.

XXXIX.

THE LAST KNOT IN THE STRING.

LANDON had scarcely uttered the words which I have just recorded, when a horseman in gray suddenly made his appearance, coming at full gallop across an extensive field west of the house.

"Look!" said Landon; "that is Touch-and-go. I sent him out to reconnoitre, and he has something to report."

"An attack, do you think?"

"It is probable. We are not far from the main camp of the enemy's cavalry."

"True; and Ratcliffe escaped; he has probably given the alarm."

"He has certainly done so."

"Then look out!"

Landon's cool smile responded.

"I expect an attack," he said; "did I not tell you this morning that to-day would be an era in my life, — would bring some singular event? Well, I think the event is coming."

And Landon rode to meet the young scout.

" You will be attacked in ten minutes, captain ! "
said Touch-and-go, quickly.

" From what quarter ? "

Touch-and-go pointed in the direction from which
he had come.

" Their number ? "

" About a hundred ! "

" Good ! that is not too many."

" Look out ! " said the scout, pointing to the
woods ; " there they are ! "

As he spoke a dark mass of blue cavalry appeared
suddenly in the edge of the wood, formed line of
battle, and came on with loud cheers.

Landon was ready. I saw in his flashing eye the
gaudium certaminis, — that fierce joy which drives
the stern soul of the born soldier to combat, bracing
his muscle for the hard struggle.

Drawing up his men in the open field near the
smoking ruin, Landon placed himself in front, gave
the order " Charge ! " and went at headlong speed to
meet the enemy.

The two lines came together with a thundering
clash. In an instant the blue and gray cavaliers
were slashing at each other furiously ; and Landon
met the assault upon his little band with a dash and
obstinacy which I had never seen in him before.

All at once, in the very middle of the mad and
whirling crowd of horsemen, — amid the hissing bul-

lets, the clashing sabres, and the trampling hoofs, — I saw the white robe of Miss Adair, and her proud, fearless face.

"Look! they are coming yonder!" she exclaimed, with extended arm.

I turned and saw a dense column of Federal cavalry approaching at full gallop over the White Post road. They were at least a hundred in number; had been evidently sent round to surprise us; and, what was worst of all, Landon, fighting the other column, did not see them, as they came thundering on to cut him off.

"For Heaven's sake, go back!" I exclaimed to Miss Adair.

And with three bounds of my horse I was beside Landon.

"Look out!" I shouted, and I pointed to the approaching column.

Landon looked, and his teeth were clenched. In his eye I saw the stern glare of the tiger at bay.

"Well," he said, in his brief tone, "there is Ratcliffe in front of them. I don't intend to retreat. We can die here."

And the Partisan turned his head and looked toward Miss Adair, who was gazing at him.

"Good!" he said; "it is something for her to see me die!"

And, throwing himself into the melée of clashing

sabres, with the fury of a wild beast, Landon shouted
to the Rangers to form line and meet the assault on
their flank.

It was too late.

The Federal reinforcement came on with trium-
phant shouts, their hoofs shaking the ground, and
among them I recognized Ratcliffe.

In an instant we were surrounded; two hundred
men, nearly, were opposed to twenty-five or thirty;
there was evidently little hope of extrication from
that fatal cordon.

Landon was fighting like a tiger, in the midst of
twenty enemies, and beside him were Arden and
Touch-and-go.

Suddenly Arden's horse was shot, and fell with
him under the trampling hoofs.

At the same moment I saw Touch-and-go totter in
the saddle and close his eyes.

I reached out my arm to hold the brave boy in his
seat, but a single glance told me that he was shot
through the heart.

He fell, half rose, and then, with a convulsive
movement, drew from his pocket the knotted string.
His fingers twitched at it; succeeded in tying a last
knot in the string; then Touch-and-go fell back,
with a childlike smile on his lips, closed his eyes,
and expired.

That was the last I saw of the combat.

Suddenly a blow from behind hurled me out of the saddle. I had a confused idea of iron hoofs within a few inches of my face; above me resounded shouts, cheers, cries of triumph, mingled with shots and sabre-strokes; then a horse's hoof struck me; I felt the blood gush over my eyes, and lost consciousness.

XL.

ACROSS A GRAVE.

WHEN I opened my eyes I was lying, bruised and bleeding, beneath a tall oak, near and directly eastward from the Old Chapel.

The sun was near its setting. The great orb glared, like a huge bloodshot eye, from beneath a low-hung and murky cloud; and this glare — crimson and threatening — lit up a strange and tragic spectacle.

Within ten paces of me, under a lofty tree, a grave had just been dug. Beside the grave, with his arms tightly bound behind him by means of his red sash, stood Landon — and opposite him, Ratcliffe. Twenty yards from them I saw Judge Adair, closely guarded, and holding clasped in his arms the form of his daughter, who had fainted. Over the slope, dotted with moss-clad rocks, were scattered the Federal cavalrymen, who had dismounted and tethered their horses to the boughs.

The situation of affairs could not be mistaken. The Night-Hawks had all been killed or dispersed; Landon and myself taken prisoner. He was bound

like a malefactor; and it was probable that, in retaliation for the bloody scene of the morning, we would
be put to death without mercy. Landon's fate
seemed certain. That grave newly dug seemed to
indicate that Ratcliffe had fully determined then and
there to put an end to his mortal enemy.

I afterwards discovered that Landon had fought to
the last, killing nearly a dozen of his assailants; but,
his horse being shot, he had fallen and been captured, when his men dispersed and escaped. The
Partisan was then bound and brought to the Old
Chapel, whither Judge Adair, his daughter, and
myself were also conducted.

My first glance, upon opening my eyes, was at
Landon. It is impossible to describe the cool courage expressed in the face of the Partisan. In his
resolute eye and lip there was no emotion whatever.
The stern nerve of the man seemed to defy the attempt to crush him, and he looked that death which
was approaching, in the face without the quiver of a
muscle. I have seen brave men in my time. I
think this one was the bravest of all.

From Landon my glance passed to Ratcliffe. His
face, habitually ruddy, had the sickly hue of a
corpse; but in the snake-like eyes there was an expression of malignant triumph which was revolt-
ing.

As I awoke to the consciousness of the scene passing before me, Ratcliffe had just advanced to the grave opposite Landon, and addressed him : —

"Are you ready?" he said, in a hoarse voice.

"I am," returned Landon, coolly.

"You know your fate?"

"To be shot, doubtless."

"And you are not afraid?"

"I am not."

The reply seemed to arouse Ratcliffe's rage to the utmost.

"Ah! you brave me!" he said.

"I reply to you," returned Landon.

"Ah! well, we will see who has the last word here! Your little game is played, — is it? Your claws are pulled! You are in my power now, and I have not yet decided whether I will shoot you or hang you!"

Landon turned livid.

"Hang me!"

"Yes."

"You dare not!"

Ratcliffe laughed savagely.

"What is to prevent me? I am in command here. I have orders from head-quarters to hang every guerilla I capture. Do you think any questions will be asked when I return and report that I caught and hung *you?*"

Landon's countenance had recovered its iron calmness. In face of this threat, so terrible to a soldier, he seemed as unmoved as before it had been uttered.

"True," he said, with his eyes fixed coolly upon Ratcliffe. "I had forgotten that your generals had become house-burners and hangmen. It is true that I might have understood it; they have always been jail-birds."

"Take care, sir!"

"And their subordinates are no better."

Ratcliffe laid his hand on his pistol, his eyes glaring.

"You suit each other," continued Landon, in a sarcastic voice; "master and man! — workman and tool! You cannot beat us; you burn houses and starve women. That is called patriotism with you; in other countries it is called cowardice!"

Ratcliffe bounded with fury.

"Beware!" he exclaimed, hoarsely, and turning white with passion.

"Beware of what?" said Landon, without moving a muscle; "why not speak my mind, since that is the only satisfaction that remains to me? You were always a cur, Ratcliffe, from the first moment that I knew you. Do you remember at Lexington when I insulted you, and you did not resent it? How at West Point, when your vulgarity had disgusted me, I told you if you spoke to me again I

would cane you? You sneaked away in silence, —
courage was not your weakness, — and you are no
better now, when you come with your ruffians to
burn the houses of Virginia over the heads of women
and children and sick people; when you break your
parole, sneak off to avoid meeting me in honourable
combat, and wreak your vengeance on a young lady
who despises you as I despise you! Pshaw! my
dear Captain Ratcliffe, you are not worth contempt.
Do you think I am cowed; that I am afraid
of you? Undeceive yourself. It is you who are
afraid of me, Ratcliffe; and the proof is that you
bind me;" — a menacing flash of the eye accompanied the words — "that you refuse the proposition
I have made you to place a sword in my hands, face
me, and fight me. No; that is not your game.
A gentleman would do that; *you* belong to the
canaille, and you tie your adversary's arms, instead
of leaving them free.

"Well, so be it! — act your character. Come,
make haste to detail your squad; give your orders.
You cannot frighten me! There is one thing you
cannot do, — frighten the man who stands before you,
bound in your power. And you feel at this moment — I see it in your eyes, Ratcliffe — that, in
life or death, St. Leger Landon is your master!"

Landon's countenance and attitude as he spoke
were full of a superb defiance. In his flaming eye

burned a stubborn and haughty courage, which nothing seemed able to affect.

Only once had the dazzling glance passed from the face of Ratcliffe to the fainting form of Miss Adair, and that glance recalling, as it did, the presence of the young lady, seemed to drive Ratcliffe to a wild fury. Words failed him. Convulsed with passion, he drew his pistol, cocked it, and growled, hoarsely : —

"Have you finished?"

" Yes," said Landon, coldly.

Ratcliffe raised his pistol.

"Good!" said Landon; "that is the nearest approach to the honourable duel I offered you. You use the pistol — at ten paces — only your adversary is bound, and cannot return your cowardly fire!"

Ratcliffe let the weapon fall.

"Fool that I am," he exclaimed, "not to understand the drift of your bravado, — to avoid the rope!" And, turning suddenly to one of his men : —

" Bring a rope halter!" he shouted.

Suddenly a young officer bounded into the area and advanced straight to Ratcliffe. It was young Lieutenant Arden, — Harry's brother, — covered with sweat and blood, his lips half opened and showing the clenched teeth, his eyes burning in his white face.

"Stop!" he said, in a voice which I scarcely recognized. "I protest in the name of every officer of the Federal army against this wanton and cowardly murder!"

XLI.

ARDEN'S BADGES.

RATCLIFFE turned like a tiger, and measured the speaker from head to foot with a glance of inexpressible wrath and surprise.

"You dare!" he exclaimed; "you presume to address your superiour officer in that tone of insubordination?"

"I dare to defend the honour of the gentlemen of the army," replied Lieutenant Arden, in a voice quivering with rage. "I dare to speak as I feel, and as every officer here present feels, and tell you that this is murder, — cold-blooded murder!"

The words raised a tumult in the crowd. For the first time the young officers attached to the command seemed to realize what was taking place before them. Ratcliffe heard that confused murmur — glared around him — was about to speak — when Lieutenant Arden interrupted him.

"I say it is murder!" he exclaimed, "to hang a gentleman, — your prisoner, — as burning that house over a sick man and a young lady was barbarous, and opposed to all the laws of civilized war-

fare! I protested against that act. I warned you,
Captain Ratcliffe, that you were dishonouring the
flag. I proceeded to the point of insubordination in
refusing to command the party, and now I do not
shrink from more, — from mutiny, if you like the
word, — only be sure of one thing, that I will not
be shot down or hanged like a dog! If I die, I will
not die alone! "

And Arden laid a furious hand on his pistol.

Ratcliffe shrunk back, recoiling from the hot eyes
and the threatening gesture.

" Come, arrest me! try me! glut your thirst for
murder! " exclaimed Arden. " I know you, and I
know the danger I am running if my brother officers
keep silent and permit you to outrage me! I expect
to be arrested, to be tried for insubordination; but
before I give up my sword you shall hear me! "

And, advancing two steps, Arden went on with
concentrated passion : —

" I entered the army of the United States to make
war on men. My aim was to help to crush the rebellion. I meant to assist in doing so by honourable
warfare, not by a base and cowardly war on women
and children. In the army the gentlemen thought
as I thought; they accepted commissions, shed their
blood, fought bravely, and died bravely, to restore
the old Union of Washington. They did not mean
to burn houses over women, and hang prisoners.

They did not mean to make the flag which they fought under a by-word. They did not mean to have ' house-burner,' and ' hangman,' and ' murderer,' stuck on to their names; and *my* name, I swear, shall not be dishonoured ! ''

As he uttered these furious words, the young man unbuckled his belt and threw his sabre at the feet of Ratcliffe. It fell with a ringing clash; and Arden exclaimed : —

" Take my sword ! I will never more draw it in a cause that is disgraced by such men as yourself, and by such acts as I have witnessed to-day ! Take my commission ! ''

And, drawing a paper from his breast, he threw it contemptuously from him.

" Take my badges of rank ! ''

And, violently tearing from his shoulders his lieutenant's straps, he hurled them to the ground, and placed his heel upon them.

" That commission," he exclaimed, " is a dishonour ! These badges would burn my shoulders if I wore them longer. I throw them down, and trample on them, and scorn them, as I scorn that flag yonder, that for three years I have fought under. It is no longer my flag. I renounce it, and will never more fight for it. Now, arrest, try, murder me, if you will. At least you cannot dishonour me.''

XLII.

"COWARD! COWARD! COWARD!"

SUDDENLY the deep voice of Landon was heard amid the silence.

"Dishonour you, — that person?" he said, looking at Ratcliffe. "You are jesting, my dear lieutenant. He can dishonour nobody."

And, turning to the group of young officers who were near: —

"Gentlemen of the Federal army," said the Partisan, with his cool, defiant smile, "I really have some curiosity to ascertain one thing, — whether you suspect the real character of this Ratcliffe? Shall I enlighten your ignorance, tell you all about him, messieurs, in a very few words? Well, your commander is a sneak, a poltroon; he betrayed his friend first; then he *broke his parole* when I, that friend whom he had tricked, captured and released him that he might fight me!"

"Impossible!" exclaimed the young officers.

"It is the truth! Look at his face! Let him dare to deny it!"

And Landon fixed his steady gaze upon Ratcliffe.

The response of that personage was to raise his pistol.

"See!" said Landon, coolly; "that is his reply to me; the reply of a poltroon, is it not? I am a West Pointer like himself, like yourselves, — and I have some of the *esprit du corps* still left; well, I am ashamed of that creature, for he dishonours not only the uniform he now wears, but that which I once wore when we were cadets."

The young Federal officers uttered a murmur. One of them stepped forth from the rest.

"Captain Ratcliffe," he said, "I have no right to question you, but you must be aware that these charges affect the honour of the officers of the Federal army in your person."

Ratcliffe scowled at the speaker with an expression of bitter menace; but it was easy to see that all the rest agreed with the young officer.

"It is a lie!" cried Ratcliffe, hoarsely.

"What is a lie?" said Landon, coolly; "that you made my acquaintance and fawned on me at Lexington? — that I introduced you into society in the Valley? — that you were a guest in my house, my associate and friend, and yet paid your addresses to the young lady who was affianced to me? Is that a lie, sir? Deny it, and the young lady is yonder, your prisoner, ready to speak. But I have not finished, I swear to you! Is it a lie, that when you

came to hate and fear me at West Point, you wrote
anonymous letters blackening my character; stole
my engagement ring from my finger whilst I was
asleep in your quarters, and, sending it to the lady,
destroyed my happiness by that cowardly treachery?
Ah, your face is pale! You shrink! You are surprised that I know that! It is not a lie, then, any
more than the statement that I captured you the
other day; paroled you to fight me; and that you
broke that parole, and escaped like a coward. Answer! Did you, or did you not, break your parole
and thus dishonour your uniform? Dare to say that
you did not, and I will appeal to the brave officer
who was to have acted as your second, Lieutenant
Arden."

And Landon pointed to Arden, who was standing
pale, disdainful, and with folded arms, in the centre
of the group.

"It is true," he said; "Captain Ratcliffe broke
his parole."

The Federal officers had gathered around the two
foes, facing each other. At those words from Arden,
they drew back from Ratcliffe, who was thus left
standing alone, avoided by all.

Landon's lip curled elaborately and with an un-
speakable expression of scorn. Slowly moving his
head in the direction of Ratcliffe: —

"Look!" he said; "he is afraid of me, bound as

I am. That is becoming — is it not, gentlemen? — in one wearing your blue uniform, and holding a commission under your Stars and Stripes."

A hoarse murmur from the group of officers greeted these disdainful words.

"I find that strange, gentlemen," said Landon, with his defiant smile, "and realize with difficulty that you tolerate such people. For, do not think, messieurs, that in the Southern army we rate you as 'mud-sills' and low people. I have always scorned to make out our enemies mere ruffians and cowards; — cowards! where were the merit of whipping you were you such? But such men as this friend of ours " — and he indicated Ratcliffe with the same disdainful movement of the head — "are apt to produce the impression that your *militaires* are *not* exactly what General Hooker calls them, 'immensely superior, intellectually and physically,' to the Southerners. When did a Southern officer break his parole and sneak from a fair combat? When did a Southern officer trick his friend, and forge, and lie? There is the man who has done all this, and he wears your blue uniform. In ten minutes — or so — he is going to shoot me, with my hands bound behind me, unarmed, because he is afraid of me, and knows that my death alone will preserve him from personal chastisement."

Ratcliffe shuddered with rage, and the second

time the trigger of his pistol clicked as he cocked it; a second time the weapon was directed at Landon.

"Look! the Partisan said, with his short, harsh laugh; "this model United States officer is going to shoot his disarmed enemy; and in all this company of Federal officers, West Pointers, there is not one to even remonstrate."

"You are wrong!" said Arden, bounding forward. And, facing Ratcliffe, with inexpressible scorn in his face, he said:—

"You attempted to dishonour me by breaking your parole yonder! You dishonour the United States flag by your cowardly cruelty here! Well, end all at once! Shoot me as well as your prisoner! You have shed my brother's blood; you have disgraced a noble cause! Life is no longer supportable to me; come, order me to be shot! But, before you do so, you cannot prevent me from branding you, in the name of the officers of this army, as coward! coward! coward!"

And, advancing a step at each repetition of the word "coward," Arden drew off his gauntlet, and was about to slap Ratcliffe in the face, when suddenly an event occurred which put an abrupt end to the scene.

XLIII.

NEMESIS.

ARDEN had scarcely uttered these words, full of vehement passion and scorn, when a shot resounded from the direction of the river.

At that ominous sound every head turned; every ear listened.

Suddenly a shout was heard; a man came over the crest at full gallop, and, darting into the midst of the cavalry men, cried : —

"Look out! the enemy are upon you!"

Ratcliffe's expression at that instant defied description. Never have I seen rage, hatred, and disappointment more vividly depicted upon the human countenance. In his eye was the savage glare of the wolf, forced to relinquish the prey which he holds between his teeth, and driven to bay by the huntsman.

By an instinctive movement, he made two steps toward his horse. Then his eye fell upon Landon, and he returned toward the grave with a bound, shouting :—

"The rope!"

But the man whom he had ordered to bring it

had hastened to mount his horse, and Ratcliffe saw that it was too late.

Beyond the crest already resounded the trampling of hoofs, the shouts of men evidently coming on at full gallop, and the crack of carbines as the assailants drove all before them.

"To horse!" shouted Ratcliffe. Then he turned to Landon.

"You are going to be rescued, you think," he cried, hoarsely. "You are wrong."

And, drawing his pistol, he aimed at Landon, and drew the trigger.

The weapon snapped, and Ratcliffe uttered a loud curse. Then, before he could again cock the weapon, I witnessed a spectacle which made the blood leap fiercely in my veins.

Landon, whose hands were still confined by the red sash behind him, cleared the grave at one bound, threw himself upon Ratcliffe, and caught him by the throat with his teeth.

The assault was so sudden that Ratcliffe could not defend himself. The teeth of the Partisan were buried in the flesh, to which they clung with the tenacity of a bloodhound.

Half strangled, with the blood spouting, with Landon's weight on his breast, Ratcliffe staggered, uttered a low cry, and fell at full length on the ground beneath his adversary.

Then a ferocious struggle took place between the two mortal enemies, who, losing sight apparently of all else, concentrated all their energies upon the conflict in which they were personally engaged.

Ratcliffe vainly attempted to tear Landon from his throat. The furious teeth still clung to the mangled and bleeding flesh ; a foam of blood encircled the lips of the Partisan as he bit deeper and deeper ; and from Ratcliffe's lips escaped a hoarse and inarticulate cry, which had in it scarcely anything that was human.

It was lost in a great uproar, which suddenly filled the air. Over the crest of the hill, from the direction of the Shenandoah, a band of Partisans appeared, — coming on at full gallop, and firing volleys at the Federal cavalrymen, who mounted their horses in hot haste. In an instant the grassy slope became the scene of a furious combat, — a chaos of smoke, dust, and blood, above which rose yells, clashing sabres, and the quick trample of hoofs.

At the head of the assailants, with drawn sabre and glowing cheeks, rode Blount. Beside him was Antoinette Duvarny, who, escaping, as I afterwards heard, from her guard at "Bizarre," had arrived at the Chapel just as Landon's men were dispersed, hastened to find Captain Blount, who she heard was near the river, and now rode at his side in the charge upon her former comrades. Of that strange meeting with him whose heart she had broken, I never heard any details.

The wild clash of arms for a moment diverted my attention from Landon and Ratcliffe. The furious struggle of the enemies now absorbed me, and I lost sight of all else.

Stretched at full length beneath his adversary, Ratcliffe vainly attempted to shake off the mortal incubus.

"Help!" I heard him mutter, as Landon's teeth dug deeper into his streaming throat. But his cry was unheard; in the wild melée he was not seen, or his fate was uncared for.

I saw on the dark face the sickly hue of despair. The lips were convulsed, the eyes protruded; the countenance of the Federal captain resembled a hideous mask rather than the face of a human being.

His hands clutched madly at the grass, which he tore up by handfuls. Writhing to and fro, dragging each other like wild animals, the bitter foes approached, foot by foot, the brink of the newly-dug grave, into which it seemed probable that they would fall, still locked in that deadly embrace.

All at once Ratcliffe uttered a cry of fierce satisfaction. His hand had fallen upon the pistol which he had dropped when Landon sprung upon him, and I saw him cock it and place the muzzle upon his adversary's breast.

I rose and staggered toward them. Then the blood rushed over my face, and I fell forward.

A report followed.

I opened my eyes, looked toward the adversaries, and saw Landon fall back, pale and covered with blood.

Ratcliffe had risen to his feet.

I shall never forget the agony of that moment, or the appearance of Ratcliffe. As pale as a corpse, his breast shaking, his throat bleeding, he glanced at Landon with an expression of diabolical triumph.

Then he threw a glance around him. That glance revealed everything. His men were breaking in the wildest disorder, and the Partisans were pursuing their flying adversaries in every direction, firing upon them, or cutting them down with the sabre.

Ratcliffe saw that all was lost; that his situation was desperate, his capture imminent; and he staggered toward a riderless horse, passing at the moment, the bridle of which he caught.

His foot was in the stirrup when a loud exclamation escaped from his lips.

Coming to meet him, and, staggering like himself, I saw Captain Blount. His face was white, and his breast bleeding. In his right hand he held a cocked pistol.

" We have met at last ! " he said, faintly.

" Blount ! " Ratcliffe cried, hoarsely.

" Yes, sir," said the captain of Partisans, in a low but deliberate voice; " the gentleman whom your baseness ruined."

" I surrender ! "

" It is too late, sir."

Ratcliffe recoiled before the pale and threatening face. Exerting all his remaining strength, he threw himself into the saddle, and dug the spur into the side of his animal.

Blount did not rush upon him as I expected. A strange smile came to his white face, and he remained as motionless as a statue.

" I am — dying — " he murmured; " but — we will — go — together."

And, raising his pistol, he took deliberate aim, and fired. As the smoke drifted, I saw that Blount had concentrated for this last act his whole remaining strength ; the pistol dropped from his grasp, and he fell forward, dead.

Ratcliffe had uttered a wild cry, and I saw his hand go to his breast, from which the blood spouted. He was still able, however, to retain his seat in the saddle, and the speed of his horse was such that he would probably have escaped, had it not been for an incident which resembled fatality.

As long as the flying animal continued his straight course, the Federal officer was evidently strong enough to retain his seat in the saddle.

Suddenly, however, a bleeding body interposed itself directly in his path. The horse snorted, and shied; and the movement decided the fate of Ratcliffe.

He was thrown, and his head struck violently against a ledge of rock. He rose, his face covered with blood, his hands clutching at the air; then falling to the earth, he writhed for a moment, and expired.

As he uttered his last groan the bleeding body which had made his horse shy, writhed, half-erect. I recognized Antoinette Duvarny and saw a strange smile upon her features. A moment afterwards her head drooped, and she was dead.

All this had passed in a few seconds. The death of Blount, and the singular end of Ratcliffe, through the instrumentality of the woman so deeply wronged by him, had riveted my whole attention, but now, all at once, the fate of Landon became my absorbing thought.

In this whirlpool of death was he also to disappear? Was his wound a mortal one? I rose and staggered toward him.

As I did so, I felt my head grow dizzy, and something in my throat seemed to choke me. Reeling to him, I caught his body in my arms, murmured "Landon!"—I could say no more,—and fell, lifeless almost, beside him.

My voice seemed to recall him from the very

17

gates of death. His eyes opened faintly, and he
looked at me with that vacant expression which
sends a pang through the heart.

" Landon ! " I repeated.

But he did not seem to hear me. His pale cheeks
had suddenly flushed, his dull eyes had grown brilliant; with a face glowing all over with an expression of heroic tenderness, he stretched his arms
faintly toward some one behind me.

" Oh, no ! " he murmured, smiling; " I am not
going to die now."

A low sob replied to him ; a light and hurried step
approached ; a moment afterwards Landon's form was
encircled by the arm of Ellen Adair, and his head
had fallen upon her bosom.

EPILOGUE.

I.

THE BLUE COURIER.

In the summer of 1865, after Lee's surrender, I paid a visit to my friend, Colonel Beverley, at his estate of " The Oaks," in Fauquier.

I hope the worthy reader will not regard the transition from 1864 to 1865, and from the fierce drama at the Old Chapel to the quiet scenes of peaceful days, as too abrupt.

You saw — did you not, my dear reader ? — that the drama ended yonder on that grassy slope near the willows of the old graveyard; that any further scenes, when the fifth act had ended, would be superfluous, and appear stale, flat, and unprofitable ? Believe me, there are few things more " fatal " than a real drama. Do you wish to stop ? — it drags you! Do you wish to go beyond the limit ? — it holds you back! When Macbeth is dead, the play ends, you see ; and there is very little to interest when Richard has carried away his hump into oblivion.

So the drama tyrannizes, but there is the friendly and more obliging Epilogue. Let us parody Sancho Panza, and say, " Blessed is the man who invented the Epilogue, — for therein may be collected all the personages and events which have been dismissed too unceremoniously in the drama ! "

I am going, therefore, worthy reader, to tell you a little more about our friends the Night-Hawks and their chief; and, as I have narrated in the preceding sheets only what I witnessed or heard, I will continue to do so in these concluding pages.

It was about the middle of April, 1865, then, when, having traversed the same road from the Rapidan northward, which I had passed over in September, 1864, I found myself — a prisoner on parole, with two horses, and the grand privilege of remaining unmolested — at " The Oaks ! " in the county of Fauquier.

I am not going to dwell upon the old homestead and the kind hearts there. Would you know all about them ? You have only to read my *Memoirs.* Many scenes of that volume occur at " The Oaks." There I first met a young lady, who is looking over my shoulder now as I write; and it was this face which I went thither to see after Appomattox Court House, even before I came hither to " Eagle's Nest " on the Rappahannock.

Observe how I try to find an excuse to tarry at

"The Oaks!" 'Tis a charming place, and the sun seems to shine brighter there than elsewhere in the world. But I must come back to the personages who have played parts in this fierce episode of my Memoirs.

My acquaintance with Landon — did you fancy him dead of his wound, reader? — was renewed in a manner the most simple.

One morning a courier, dressed in *blue*, came to "The Oaks," with a note from the Federal officer commanding just over the ridge. Would I oblige him by repairing on the next morning, if convenient, to Millwood? He was anxious to obtain from me, as an officer from General Lee's head-quarters, details relating to the precise manner in which General Grant had paroled the Confederate forces; the work in hand being to parole the Partisans of the Shenandoah.

My blue friend — how familiar and like "old times" already, he looked! — was exceedingly deferential, and waited, with his hand to his cap, for a reply. I wrote it; he saluted and disappeared. On the next morning I mounted my horse and set out for Ashby's Gap.

This time there were no Confederates on the fence of the old tavern at Paris — no videttes at the ford of the Shenandoah — no Night-Hawks or blue people on picket anywhere.

But a mile further I saw them; and in the streets of Millwood were my old friends of the night, mingling with Federal cavalrymen in charming fellowship. They were laughing, joking, and jesting at each other; and at the head of the Night-Hawks was Landon.

II.

THE Partisan greeted me with cordial warmth, and introduced me to the commander of the Federal forces, with whom I proceeded to converse upon the business which had brought me.

"We have agreed on a truce till twelve to-day," said Landon, when I had finished, "and if by that time we do not settle terms of surrender, I am to go with my Night-Hawks to open the war again."

"You shall not be forced to do that, captain," said the Federal officer, whose tone was perfectly courteous.

And the negotiations commenced.

At twelve they were not concluded, and Landon mounted his horse.

"Form column!" he said to his men, "and unroll the flag!"

At the word the Night-Hawks sprung to horse, and the red battle-flag of the Confederacy floated proudly in the wind.

Never shall I forget my feelings as I saw that banner again given to the air! I had seen it furled on the Appomattox; I now saw it unrolled again on the Shenandoah! My heart throbbed, and my hand went to my side, feeling for the sabre.

Alas! there was none there. But I went and "fell in" by Landon.

The Federal cavalry had sprung to horse at the moment when Landon mounted. The men in blue and gray, but a moment before jesting with each other, laid their hands upon their sword-hilts.

For the last time I saw the gray ranks face the blue in line of battle; for the last time the red-cross flag flaunt proudly in the face of the Stars and Stripes!

"Forward!" trembled on Landon's lips, and his eye flashed.

What would have happened, I know not; but at that moment hoof-strokes were heard upon the turnpike; a courier came at full gallop from the direction of Winchester; and the next instant the Federal officer in command was reading a dispatch.

As he finished, he bowed to Landon, and said : —

"I am glad to inform you, captain, that General Hancock has extended the truce until sunset this evening, and the Partisan troops are placed upon the same footing as General Lee's army. They will be paroled on the same terms."

Landon bowed gloomily.

"I accept the terms of parole for my command," he said.

And, breaking ranks by his order, the men formally surrendered and were paroled, retaining their horses and side-arms.

Then, without word, they mounted and formed line. All eyes were turned to Landon; it was plain that they were waiting for his last words to them.

He spurred forward, his head erect, his eye flashing, his keen glance running along the line, as though to see that it was "dressed."

Then, removing his hat, he spoke.

I will not attempt to repeat his words. I could do so, for they thrilled through me. Again my heart throbbed hotly. I recall every word, every accent, and every expression of the face of the Partisan.

As he spoke, the rough Rangers stirred and murmured. With flushed faces and flashing eyes, they seemed to go back and live over the glorious days when they chased the very blue horsemen now before them.

Landon ended his brief and fiery address in a few minutes. Then, turning with an electric gesture toward the red flag which one of the men had seized and unrolled, he drew his sword, and said in his deep, proud voice: —

"I salute the flag which history will salute forever!"

A whirl of the arm — the sabre at a salute, in which the whole band imitated him — a burst of cheers — and the Night-Hawks looked at Landon.

" Break ranks ! " he said.

And, as he spurred into their midst, the men seized his hand, his coat, and seemed utterly unable to control the wild sobs that burst from them.

In another instant the Partisan had made me a sign, and we were proceeding at a full gallop toward " Bizarre."

III.

I saw that Landon's emotion was nearly choking him, and did not utter a word.

We passed on rapidly, entered the forest, swept along beneath the great oaks, and suddenly came in sight of "Bizarre."

Then, as we approached, I saw all at once the gleam of a robe at the great gate. A form hastened to meet us, the sweet eyes full of tears. Landon sprung from his horse, and catching the young lady in his arms, allowed his head to fall upon her shoulder.

"I have surrendered!" he said, hoarsely. "I was obliged to, on my men's account."

And for the first time a fiery tear dimmed his eye.

"It is hard, — is it not, colonel?" he said with his proud head raised, and a faint smile upon his lips; "it makes children of us old soldiers!"

Then, taking the lady's hand he held it out to me and said: —

"You know Mrs. Landon!"

It was Ellen Adair's bright eyes which looked at me, her warm hand which pressed mine, her smiling lips which greeted me ; and we walked on, in pleasant talk, to the old mansion.

"Bizarre" was still "torn down" and war-worn in appearance, — but all our Virginia homes were thus in '65. The old mansion seemed to smile upon us, nevertheless, as we approached ; the great door stood hospitably open. As we entered the hall, the old portraits, in lace and powder, on the dim canvas, seemed to smile, but not so brightly as the lovely face of Ellen Adair, as I will still call her, who was beside me.

Then, all at once, there came out of the parlour to meet us, a charming maiden of seventeen or eighteen, who approached and gave me her hand. It was Miss Annie Meadows, full of smiles and blushes, and behind her came, limping, and leaning on his brother Ralph, no less a personage than my dear Harry Arden.

So you see, reader, nobody that was worth living was dead, except the noble Blount and the brave Touch-and-go. And even they — they sleep, but are not dead !

Harry Arden had been desperately wounded, but was brought with Landon after the fight to "Bizarre," where I left them to return to Petersburg. Landon had soon recovered, and had been married for a month. Harry was nearly well ; and it was plain that "Annie" had been "thinking" a great deal of him, and was soon going to become Mrs. Arden. As to Ralph, he had never again entered the army; had returned to Delaware; put on citizens' clothes; was on a visit to his brother now, and gave me one of the most cordial pressures of the hand I ever received.

An hour afterwards, Landon and myself had strolled to Lover's Leap. From the shadowy pine wood came a pensive sigh; the murmur of the Shenandoah ascended to the great rock; and on the slopes of the Blue Ridge the red sunset fell in mellow splendour.

Landon leaned against the solitary pine and mused. The hour subdued me too, and, resting my head upon my hand, I fell into a reverie. They were bitter — those reveries — in April, '65, friend. Did you dream then, as we did? I have had pleasanter dreams.

Landon sighed as he gazed on the splendid landscape.

"Surrender! — the flag lowered!" I heard him murmur, — "we have lost all."

"But me!"

And a form passed me, two tender arms clasped him; the head of Ellen Adair was resting upon his heart.

A week afterwards I was at Eagle's Nest.

And in this spring of 1868, I have found time to write the history of St. Leger Landon.

May you like it, my dear reader !

SURRY OF EAGLE'S NEST.

THE END.

NEW BOOKS
And New Editions Recently Published by
CARLETON, Publisher,
NEW YORK.

N.B.—The Publishers, upon receipt of the price in advance, will send any of the following Books by mail, postage free, to any part of the United States. This convenient and very safe mode may be adopted when the neighboring Book sellers are not supplied with the desired work. State name and address in full.

Victor Hugo.

LES MISÉRABLES.—The celebrated novel. One large 8vo volume, paper covers, $2.00 ; . . . cloth bound, $2.50

LES MISÉRABLES.—In the Spanish language. Fine 8vo. edition, two vols., paper covers, $4.00 ; . . cloth bound, $5.00

JARGAL.—A new novel. Illustrated. . 12mo. cloth, $1.75

THE LIFE OF VICTOR HUGO.—By himself. . 8vo. cloth, $1.75

Miss Muloch.

JOHN HALIFAX.—A novel. With illustration. 12mo. cloth, $1.75

A LIFE FOR A LIFE.— . do. do. $1.75

Charlotte Bronte (Currer Bell).

JANE EYRE.—A novel. With illustration. 12mo cloth, $1.75

THE PROFESSOR.— do. . do. . do. $1.75

SHIRLEY.— . do. . do. . do. $1.75

VILLETTE.— . do. . do. . do. $1.75

Hand-Books of Society.

THE HABITS OF GOOD SOCIETY; with thoughts, hints, and anecdotes, concerning nice points of taste, good manners, and the art of making oneself agreeable. The most entertaining work of the kind. . . . 12mo. cloth, $1.75

THE ART OF CONVERSATION.—With directions for self-culture. A sensible and instructive work, that ought to be in the hands of every one who wishes to be either an agreeable talker or listener. . . . . 12mo. cloth, $1.50

ARTS OF WRITING, READING, AND SPEAKING.—An excellent book for self-instruction and improvement . . 12mo, cloth, $1.50

HAND-BOOKS OF SOCIETY.—The above three choice volumes are also bound in extra style, full gilt ornamental back, uniform in appearance. and put up in a handsome box. Price for the set of three, ... $5.00

Algernon Charles Swinburne.

LAUS VENERIS, AND OTHER POEMS.— . 12mo, cloth, $1.75

Mrs. Mary J. Holmes' Works.

'LENA RIVERS.— . . .	A novel.	12mo. cloth,	$1.50
DARKNESS AND DAYLIGHT.— .	do. .	do. .	$1.50
TEMPEST AND SUNSHINE — .	do. .	do. .	$1.50
MARIAN GREY.— . . .	do. .	do. .	$1.50
MEADOW BROOK.— . . .	do. .	do. .	$1 50
ENGLISH ORPHANS.— . .	do. .	do. .	$1.50
DORA DEANE.— . . .	do. .	do. .	$1.50
COUSIN MAUDE.— . .	do. .	do. .	$1.50
HOMESTEAD ON THE HILLSIDE.—	do. .	do. .	$1.50
HUGH WORTHINGTON.— . .	do. .	do. .	$1.50
THE CAMERON PRIDE.— . .	do. .	do. .	$1.50
ROSE MATHER.—*Just Published.*	do. .	do. .	$1.50

Miss Augusta J. Evans.

BEULAH.—A novel of great power. .	12mo. cloth,	$1.75
MACARIA.— do. do. . .	do. .	$1.75
ST. ELMO.— do. do. *Just Published.*	do. .	$2.00

By the Author of "Rutledge."

RUTLEDGE.—A deeply interesting novel.	12mo. cloth,	$1.75
THE SUTHERLANDS.— do. . .	do. .	$1.7!
FRANK WARRINGTON.— do. . .	do. .	$1.75
ST. PHILIP'S.— do. . .	do. .	$1.75
LOUIE'S LAST TERM AT ST. MARY'S.— .	do. .	$1.75
ROUNDHEARTS AND OTHER STORIES.—For children.	do. .	$1.75
A ROSARY FOR LENT.—Devotional Readings.	do. .	$1.75

Captain Mayne Reid's Works—Illustrated.

THE SCALP HUNTERS.—	A romance.	12mo. cloth,	$1.75
THE RIFLE RANGERS.— .	do. .	do. .	$1.75
THE TIGER HUNTER.— .	do. .	do. .	$1.75
OSCEOLA, THE SEMINOLE.— .	do. .	do. .	$1.75
THE WAR TRAIL.— .	do. .	do .	$1.75
THE HUNTER'S FEAST.— .	do. .	do. .	$1.75
RANGERS AND REGULATORS.—	do. .	do. .	$1.75
THE WHITE CHIEF — .	do. .	do. .	$1.75
THE QUADROON.— .	do. .	do. .	$1.75
THE WILD HUNTRESS.— .	do. .	do. .	$1.75
THE WOOD RANGERS.— .	do. .	do. .	$1.75
WILD LIFE.— . . .	do. .	do. .	$1.75
THE MAROON.— .	do. .	do. .	$1.75
LOST LEONORE.—	do. .	do. .	$1.75
THE HEADLESS HORSEMAN.—	do. .	do. .	$1.75
THE WHITE GAUNTLET.— *Just Published.*	do. .	$1.75

A. S. Roe's Works.

A LONG LOOK AHEAD.—   A novel.   12mo. cloth, $1.50
TO LOVE AND TO BE LOVED.—   do. . .   do. $1.50
TIME AND TIDE.—   do. . .   do. $1.50
I'VE BEEN THINKING.—   do. . .   do. $1.50
THE STAR AND THE CLOUD.—   do. . .   do. $1.50
TRUE TO THE LAST.—   do. . .   do. $1.50
HOW COULD HE HELP IT?—   do. . .   do. $1.50
LIKE AND UNLIKE.—   do. . .   do. $1.50
LOOKING AROUND.—   do. . .   do. $1.50
WOMAN OUR ANGEL.—   do. . .   do. $1.50
THE CLOUD ON THE HEART.—   .   do. $1.50

Orpheus C. Kerr.

THE ORPHEUS C. KERR PAPERS.—Three vols.   12mo. cloth, $1.50
SMOKED GLASS.—New comic book.   Illustrated.   do. $1.50
AVERY GLIBUN.—A powerful new novel.—   8vo. cloth, $2.00

Richard B. Kimball.

WAS HE SUCCESSFUL?—   A novel.   12mo. cloth, $1.75
UNDERCURRENTS.—   do. . .   do. $1.75
SAINT LEGER.—   do. . .   do. $1.75
ROMANCE OF STUDENT LIFE.—do. . .   do. $1.75
IN THE TROPICS.—   do. . .   do. $1.75
HENRY POWERS, Banker.—*Just Published.*   do. $1.75

Comic Books—Illustrated.

ARTEMUS WARD, His Book.—Letters, etc.   12mo. cl., $1.50
DO.   His Travels—Mormons, etc.   do. $1.50
DO.   In London.—Punch Letters.   do. $1.50
JOSH BILLINGS ON ICE, and other things.—   do. $1.50
DO.   His Book of Proverbs, etc.   do. $1.50
WIDOW SPRIGGINS.—By author "Widow Bedott." do. $1.75
FOLLY AS IT FLIES.—By Fanny Fern.   . .   do. $1.50
CORRY O'LANUS.—His views and opinions.   . do. $1.50
VERDANT GREEN.—A racy English college story. do. $1.50
CONDENSED NOVELS, ETC.—By F. Bret Harte.   do. $1.50
THE SQUIBOB PAPERS.—By John Phœnix.   . do. $1.50
MILES O'REILLY.—His Book of Adventures.   . do. $1.50
DO.   Baked Meats, etc.   . do. $1.75

"Brick" Pomeroy.

SENSE.—An illustrated vol. of fireside musings.   12mo. cl., $1.50
NONSENSE.—   do.   do.   comic sketches.   do. $1.50

Joseph Rodman Drake.

THE CULPRIT FAY.—A faery poem.   . .   12mo. cloth, $1.25
THE CULPRIT FAY.—An illustrated edition.   100 exquisite illustrations. . . 4to., beautifully printed and bound. $5.00

Children's Books—Illustrated.

THE ART OF AMUSING.—With 150 illustrations. 12mo. cl., $1.50
FRIENDLY COUNSEL FOR GIRLS.—A charming book. do. $1.50
THE CHRISTMAS FONT.—By Mary J. Holmes. do. $1.00
ROBINSON CRUSOE.—A Complete edition. . do. $1.50
LOUIE'S LAST TERM.—By author " Rutledge. do. $1.75
ROUNDHEARTS, and other stories.— do. . do. $1.75
PASTIMES WITH MY LITTLE FRIENDS.— . . do. $1.50
WILL-O'-THE-WISP.—From the German. . do. $1.50

M. Michelet's Remarkable Works.

LOVE (L'AMOUR).—Translated from the French. 12mo. cl., $1.50
WOMAN (LA FEMME).— . do. . . do. $1.50

Ernest Renan.

THE LIFE OF JESUS.—Translated from the French. 12mo.cl.,$1.75
THE APOSTLES.— . . do. . . do. $1.75

Popular Italian Novels.

DOCTOR ANTONIO.—A love story. By Ruffini. 12mo. cl., $1.75
BEATRICE CENCI.—By Guerrazzi, with portrait. do. $1.75

Rev. John Cumming, D.D., of London.

THE GREAT TRIBULATION.—Two series. 12mo. cloth, $1.50
THE GREAT PREPARATION.— do. . do. $1.50
THE GREAT CONSUMMATION. do. . do. $1.50
THE LAST WARNING CRY.— . . do. $1.50

Mrs. Ritchie (Anna Cora Mowatt).

FAIRY FINGERS.—A capital new novel. . 12mo. cloth, $1.75
THE MUTE SINGER.— do. . do. $1.75
THE CLERGYMAN'S WIFE—and other stories. do. $1.75

Mother Goose for Grown Folks.

HUMOROUS RHYMES for grown people. . 12mo. cloth, 1 .25

T. S. Arthur's New Works.

LIGHT ON SHADOWED PATHS.—A novel. 12mo. cloth, $1.50
OUT IN THE WORLD.— . do. . . do. $1.50
NOTHING BUT MONEY.— . do. . . do. $1.50
WHAT CAME AFTERWARDS.— do. . . do. $1.50
OUR NEIGHBORS.— . do. . . do. $1.50

Geo. W. Carleton.

OUR ARTIST IN CUBA.—With 50 comic illustrations. . $1.50
OUR ARTIST IN PERU.— do. do. . . $1.50
OUR ARTIST IN AFRICA.—(*In press*) do. . . $1.50

John Esten Cooke.

FAIRFAX.—A Virginian novel. . . 12mo. cloth, $1.75
HILT TO HILT.— A Virginian novel. do. $1.50

How to Make Money

AND HOW TO KEEP IT.—A practical, readable book, that ought to be in the hands of every person who wishes to earn money or to keep what he has. One of the best books ever published. By Thomas A. Davies.   12mo. cloth, $1.50

J. Cordy Jeaffreson.

A BOOK ABOUT LAWYERS.—A collection of interesting anecdotes and incidents connected with the most distinguished members of the Legal Profession.   .   12mo. cloth, $2.00

Fred. Saunders.

WOMAN, LOVE, AND MARRIAGE.—A charming volume about three most fascinating topics.   .   .   12mo. cloth, $1.50

Edmund Kirke.

AMONG THE PINES.—Or Life in the South.   12mo. cloth, $1.50
MY SOUTHERN FRIENDS.—   do.   .   .   do. $1.50
DOWN IN TENNESSEE.—   do.   .   .   do. $1.50
ADRIFT IN DIXIE.—   do.   .   .   do. $1.50
AMONG THE GUERILLAS.—   do.   .   .   do. $1.50

Charles Reade.

THE CLOISTER AND THE HEARTH.—A magnificent new novel— the best this author ever wrote.   .   8vo. cloth, $2.00

The Opera.

TALES FROM THE OPERAS.—A collection of clever stories, based upon the plots of all the famous operas. 12mo. cloth, $1.50

Robert B. Roosevelt.

THE GAME-FISH OF THE NORTH.—Illustrated. 12mo. cloth, $2.00
SUPERIOR FISHING.—   do.   do. $2.00
THE GAME-BIRDS OF THE NORTH.—   .   .   do. $2.00

Love in Letters.

A collection of piquant love-letters, selected from the amatory correspondence of the most celebrated and rotorious men and women of History.   By J. G. Wilson.   . $2.00

Dr. J. J. Craven.

THE PRISON-LIFE OF JEFFERSON DAVIS.—Incidents and conversations during his captivity. 12mo. cloth.   . $2.00

Walter Barrett, Clerk.

THE OLD MERCHANTS OF NEW YORK —Piquant personal incidents, bits of biography, estimates of wealth, and interesting events in the lives of nearly all the leading Merchants of New York City.   Four volumes.   12mo. cloth, $1.75

H. T. Sperry.

COUNTRY LOVE vs. CITY FLIRTATION.—An amusing, satirical Society poem, illustrated with twenty superb full-page drawings by Augustus Hoppin.   .   12mo. cloth, $2.00

Miscellaneous Works.

WARWICK.—A novel by Mansfield Tracy Walworth . $1.75
REGINA, and other Poems.—By Eliza Cruger. . . $1.50
THE WICKEDEST WOMAN IN NEW YORK.—By C. H. Webb . 50
MONTALBAN.—A new American novel. . . . $1.75
MADEMOISELLE MERQUEM.—A novel by George Sand . $1.75
THE IMPENDING CRISIS OF THE SOUTH.—By H. R. Helper . $2.00
NOJOQUE—A Question for a Continent.— do. . $2.00
TEMPLE HOUSE.—A novel by Elizabeth Stoddard. . $1.75
PARIS IN 1867.—By Henry Morford. . . . $1.75
THE BISHOP'S SON.—A novel by Alice Cary. . . $1.75
CRUISE OF THE ALABAMA AND SUMTER.—By Capt. Semmes, $2.00
HELEN COURTENAY.—A novel, author "Vernon Grove." $1.75
SOUVENIRS OF TRAVEL.—By Madame Octavia W. LeVert. $2.00
VANQUISHED.—A novel by Agnes Leonard. . . $1.75
WILL-O'-THE-WISP.—A child's book, from the German . $1.50
FOUR OAKS.—A novel by Kamba Thorpe. . . . $1.75
THE CHRISTMAS FONT.—A child's book, by M. J. Holmes. $1.00
ALICE OF MONMOUTH.—By Edmund C. Stedman. . $1.50
THE LOST CAUSE REGAINED.—By Edward A. Pollard. . $1.50
MALBROOK.—A new American novel. . . . $1.75
POEMS, BY SARAH T. BOLTON. $1.50
LIVES OF JOHN S. MOSBY AND MEN.—With portraits. . $1.75
THE SHENENDOAH.—History of the Confederate Cruiser. $1.50
MARY BRANDEGEE.—A novel by Cuyler Pine. . . $1.75
RENSHAWE— do. do. . $1.75
MEMORIALS OF JUNIUS BRUTUS BOOTH—(The Elder Actor). $1.50
MOUNT CALVARY.—By Matthew Hale Smith. . . $2.00
LOVE-LIFE OF DR. ELISHA K. KANE AND MARGARET FOX. . $1.75
PROMETHEUS IN ATLANTIS.—A prophecy. . . . $2.00
TITAN AGONISTES.—An American novel. . . . $2.00
CHOLERA.—A handbook on its treatment and cure. . $1.00
THE MONTANAS.—A novel by Sallie J. Hancock. . $1.75
PASTIMES WITH LITTLE FRIENDS.—Martha Haines Butt. $1.50
LIFE OF JAMES STEPHENS.—The Fenian Head-Centre. $1.00
TREATISE ON DEAFNESS.—By Dr. E. B. Lighthill. . $1.50
AROUND THE PYRAMIDS.—By Gen. Aaron Ward. . $1.00
CHINA AND THE CHINESE.—By W. L. G. Smith. . $1.50
EDGAR POE AND HIS CRITICS.—By. Mrs. Whitman. . $1.00
MARRIED OFF.—An Illustrated Satirical Poem. . . 50
THE RUSSIAN BALL.— do. do. . . 50
THE SNOBLACE BALL.— do. do. . . 50
AN ANSWER TO HUGH MILLER.—By Thomas A. Davies $1.50
COSMOGONY.—By Thomas A. Davies. . . . $2.00
RURAL ARCHITECTURE.—By M. Field. Illustrated. . $2.00

www.ingramcontent.com/pod-product-compliance
Lightning Source LLC
Chambersburg PA
CBHW030633030726
47497CB00006B/1770